FLORALIE,
WHERE
ARE YOU?

FLORALIE, WHERE ARE YOU?

ROCH CARRIER

TRANSLATED BY SHEILA FISCHMAN

ANANSI 1971 TORONTO

Published with the assistance of the Canada Council.

Floralie, ou est tu? was first published in 1969 by
Editions du Jour, 1651, rue Saint-Denis, Montréal.

Cover design by Roland Giguère

House of Anansi Press Limited
471 Jarvis Street
Toronto 284, Canada

ISBN: 0 88784 317 4 (paper) / 0 88784 417 0 (cloth)
Library of Congress Card Number: 75-152413

Printed in Canada by the Hunter Rose Company

Translator's Foreword

Roch Carrier's second novel, *Floralie, Where Are You?* is technically a sequel to *La Guerre, Yes Sir!* but it is possible that readers of *La Guerre* may not recognize in Anthyme Corriveau and his young bride Floralie the elderly couple whose dead son, his coffin draped in the British flag and carried by English soldiers, provided the occasion for an ironic confrontation with death during the long winter night of *La Guerre*. For the sequel takes us back some thirty years; the season is spring, not winter; and the occasion is a wedding night, not a wake. But just as death may ask what it is that joins us together, love may ask what it is that divides. Night again sets the scene for much of the action. It is the time when our inner life reveals itself best in dream or nightmare. So the night here separates and tests and discovers the characters, to themselves and to the reader. The result is a kind of medieval comedy dramatizing conflicts characteristic not only of the experience of Quebeckers of a generation past but of that perennial mixture of dream and reality we call life.

Floralie, Where Are You? indicates, perhaps more clearly than *La Guerre, Yes Sir!* that Roch Carrier is no sociologist. He is not a realist except in the sense that the classic folk tale, in its primitive and sometimes ribald action and in its delineation of essential types, is realistic. And he writes in a style that has something of the classic purity and simplicity of the tale. Thus, though some English-language reviewers have spoken of Carrier's use of "joual" in *La Guerre, Yes Sir!* they are mistaken. Some writers, like the poet Gérald Godin and the novelist Jacques Renaud, may employ "joual," partly to make a political statement. Carrier does not. He sees "joual" as a degradation of his language and, although his characters may *speak* that way, he leaves it to the reader to *hear* the accent and the mispronunciation. A real-life Anthyme may call his horse (cheval) a "joual," but that's not Roch Carrier's doing. (If he were writing in English he probably wouldn't write "hoss" either.)

The young Anthyme has not yet developed into the virtuoso blasphemer of *La Guerre, Yes Sir!* He directs a remarkable variation on a biblical harangue to an unresponsive deity, but his cursing is mostly limited to "hostie," the sacred host. Here, as in *La Guerre*, swear words have not been translated, and for the same reason.

The kind of Catholicism that was until not too long ago one of the strongest forces in Québec is very evident here. The name of the priest, Father Nombrillet, is significant. "Nombril" means navel, and the name might suggest the rather narrow range of much clerical contemplation of the time. Some readers will be troubled by what may seem to be an exaggerated preoccupation with images of hell and damnation, but to the Roman Catholic Québécois these are very real, an important part of their spiritual or, if you will, "folkloric" formation.

Ingmar Bergman is another artist who deals with specific religious concerns and uses his own northern landscape to make statements with universal relevance and appeal. Just as his films are not exclusively Swedish, so Carrier is not *exclusively* a Québec writer. Still it is Québec that gives to his work its particular flair. In any human society there will be those who see in change, the coming of the railway, a threat to the moral order, the work of the devil and of foreigners. But they will not all be like the local politician who unwittingly sees his fellow citizens as cows, stampeded by the train, and sees in the train the diabolical designs of the "maudits Anglais." It is the ironic incarnation of the type, the play of the novel and the conventional, in which the reader delights. And in this instance, perhaps no reader more than the *maudit Anglais* himself.

S.F.

The horse was restless in its collar; the traces were irritating its flanks. It stomped, trying to pull the buggy whose four wheels were squealing on their axles. With one strong hand on the bridle, Anthyme Corriveau kept the horse from moving its head.

Shirts soaked, collars open, hair damp, the wedding guests looked happily at the departing couple.

"The horse farted," announced the idiot boy with a blissful grin.

"You hear that, daughter?" asked Ernest. "The horse is wishing you *bon voyage* too."

The wedding guests danced happily on their drunken legs, until their laughter was exhausted.

"Mama," Floralie complained, "I don't feel right in this dress. I wish you'd let me wear my white one. A black dress isn't a wedding dress. If I don't wear my wedding dress today I'll never get another chance."

"The road will be rough," replied her mother, in a voice that would not tolerate argument.

Anthyme climbed into the buggy. "Thanks a lot, father-in-law, for giving me your daughter. We'll come back in a few years with our children."

"May the good Lord help you!" Ernest prayed.

"None of that! The good Lord'll never set foot on my land to help me pull up stumps."

The wedding guests greeted this blasphemy with laughs that welled up from the depths of their being. The men laughed at their wives, who had been offended by the words, and swallowed great mouthfuls of a yellowish liquid swimming with dandelions, raisins and brownish apples.

"Two arms, it's a man; but God is God," Ernest pronounced in a reproachful tone.

Anthyme pulled hard on the reins, which he held in his left hand while his right whipped the animal's hindquarters. "Get moving!"

The wheels made practically no noise on the muddy road. Standing erect, with all the majesty of a man dominating a beast, Anthyme abused his horse. The end of his whip stung harder and harder. The family and guests watched as the buggy reached the top of the hill and then disappeared into a cloud of dust.

"He couldn't wait to see the last of us," said Ernest sadly.

"Don't talk like that. You know where words like that come from, but you don't know how far they travel."

"Floralie's always been hard. You saw — she didn't even cry."

The guests had turned their backs on the newlyweds and were going towards the grey wooden house. The women were all talking at once, all with the same sharp voice; as for the men, flask or glass in hand, they needed only laughter to understand each other.

"If I'd had the chance to marry Floralie," one of them said, "I wouldn't have waited till late afternoon to disappear into the woods."

Another, the only one who was still looking towards the top of the hill, said, "Floralie wasn't for us."

Waving his flask, a boy from the village shouted in a

loud voice which Floralie, however, could not hear, "I hope you'll be miserable with your foreigner from the mountains."

"It's true, you know, the land we come from's as flat as the palm of your hand," commented another.

Floralie's father came up to the one who had wished his daughter bad luck. He snatched away his bottle and turned it over, letting the drink gurgle out. As he replaced the empty bottle in the man's hand he said, "I hope my land never gets as dry as your heart."

Ernest rubbed his hands together as though to clean them, then went off towards the stable.

The cows, their udders heavy, were mooing, expecting to be milked. Ernest kicked one on the shin. "Shut up! I want to be able to hear myself think."

His footsteps resounded on the wood floor between the two rows of stalls. His Sunday shoes could not avoid the cow pies or the urine-soaked straw. He spat pensively.

"*Baptême!* I didn't even get a chance to talk to Floralie. Anyway, my girl, I'm going to tell you what I wanted to say. You aren't here, but you're my daughter, so you'll hear me just the same as if you were. So listen: Floralie, if your soul is clean like the nice cloth on your wedding table, and if you work like your mother Mathilda, and then if you don't forget that a man's got to eat and he needs his woman to look after him, and if your husband's a little bit like your father, I promise you'll be happy. Not like a fish in water maybe, but like a married woman. Then, don't count the children . . . "

Tears were coming to his rough wrinkled eyelids.

"*Baptême!* This stable sure stinks today."

As he left the stable Ernest was blinded by the light. "I'm going to drink more than I ought to."

3

*   *   *

Floralie did not turn her head to see the village getting farther away behind her. She said, "Anthyme, I'm scared."

She wanted him to ask her why, to say, "With me you don't need to be scared; I'm strong." But he was silent. His whip lashed out at the horse. Then, after a long silence, without turning towards her, he explained, "If we want to get there before night we're going to have to move faster than the sun. Giddyup!"

A little farther on he let himself fall onto the seat near his wife. The ashy smell of strong soap that had disgusted Floralie all day had disappeared under the stronger smell of a man. Anthyme's shirt was soaked from driving his horse so hard.

"Anthyme," she insisted, "I'm afraid to be going on my wedding trip in this black dress. Mama said it's because of the dust, but as far as I'm concerned you only wear a black dress when you're in mourning. And mourning, that goes against life."

"A man never looks at a dress, he looks at what's under it. *Hostie!*"

Anthyme began to laugh and he could not stop. He stood up, whipped the horse, sat down again, fastened the reins to the apron of the buggy and then roughly put his arm around his wife's shoulders, his fingers in her armpit. He spread his other hand on Floralie's bosom and pressed his hairy face against her cheek. His big brown fingers groped furiously at her firm flesh as though he were trying to put out a fire.

"Oh! That hurts!" she groaned.

As the horse galloped the wheels whined. Floralie listen to the noise but Anthyme heard nothing.

Floralie moved nervously, trying to dislodge her husband's hand. Its big fingers seemed to be embedded in her bosom.

"You're hurting me!"

Anthyme did not want to hear. Floralie put her soft hand on her husband's and dug her nails into it.

He loosened his embrace. The blood made four red lines.

"Blood! I don't like that!"

He got up and cracked his whip on the horse, which could not run any faster.

A road had been formed in the turf by the action of cart wheels repeatedly turning in the same place. First there was underbrush. Grass grew thickly, high and wild. Where the road was, the grass bent over, trampled down; it masked damp ground that had been torn up by wheels. There were ruts where horses had tramped heavily, trying to pull a buggy out of the mud. There were still large brown spots of mud under the grass. Then the road entered the forest, climbing among black spruce trees. Twisted and shaken by the bumpy turnings, Anthyme's buggy was complaining on all sides and Floralie was afraid it would break like an egg. Anthyme kept lashing out at the horse. At every turn they could see black spruce branches spread out ahead of them. Anthyme avoided them all by pulling on one rein or the other, with a cry that hurt Floralie's ears each time she heard it. When the buggy turned on two wheels she clutched the seat. At that speed Anthyme would not be able to avoid all the spruce trees spread out at every turn in the road; they would hit a tree. Then what would happen to the buggy? It would split open like a nut under a hammer, the horse would roll whinnying into the thicket, its legs crushed. What would happen to Anthyme? And who would come to rescue her in that forest, where she would not have the strength to shout? As a matter of fact, no one would be able to hear her at all: the too heavy silence would stifle her cries, the silent spruce would hold her voice in their black branches from which mute birds flew out.

Anthyme was breathing as noisily as his panic-stricken horse.

"Apparently," Floralie thought, "men go crazy on their wedding day."

*　　*　　*

Because of the veil of branches over their heads Floralie saw the sky only as flashes of blue; it seemed to be swimming among the branches, appearing and then disappearing in a black cloud. She stopped looking at the horse and raised her eyes to the sky. As the wheels turned and the buggy jolted frantically along the road, Floralie felt the earth moving farther and farther away from the sky, the road sloping down so abruptly that she felt dizzy, as if someone were squeezing her throat.

Floralie had waited for this day so she could say, "I love you." She had waited until this day to light the little flame at the tip of her lips that would illumine her whole life. She had said it to herself, in a low voice, for herself alone, repeating it carefully so that she would learn to say it well when the time came to ignite the precious little flame that only death would extinguish. She had often repeated it as she repeated her prayers. Now that the day had come to say out loud, "I love you," the only words her lips could form were, "I'm scared, Anthyme."

How could he hear those stammered words that were lost among the grinding noise of the buggy, the cries of iron striking the pebbles, and the smothered sound of the horse's hooves pounding the ground? He was panting as if he were running in place of the animal.

Floralie looked down. She had no desire to say "I love you" to this man standing in front of her, his behind on a level with her face, his legs bent in his crumpled trousers.

She said nothing; she was dreaming about her parents' house with its good smell of hot milk. She was afraid. She held on to her seat so tightly that she almost tore the flesh of her little hand.

*   *   *

She used to like the well-combed horses' manes. She used to amuse herself by putting flowers in them and saying, "You're beautiful; you're the most beautiful of all" if it were a mare. But Floralie did not want to put flowers in the mane of Anthyme's horse. It was all standing up, tangled and shaking as the wind whipped it about. She would not have had the courage to put her hand in that furious mane.

Several times in her father's village she had seen horses with their manes ablaze. It often happened that an angry horse would rear up and bolt through the village like a streak of lightning. It would overturn everything, ramming and breaking other carriages and wagons. All kinds of things would roll through the streets — potatoes, jugs of molasses, jars of preserves, nails, rolls of fence-wire. The horse would overturn its own carriage and drag it along in a cloud of dust. It would snort, standing on its hind legs like a man, and drive its hooves into the white picket fence, neighing. The men would think that the horse was worn out; the braver ones would leave the women and children inside and appear silently on each side of the road. The horse would whirl round and round as though it wanted to tear out, with its teeth, the weight of the carriage behind it. Failing to do so it jumped, it leaped in the dust to trample its burden and suddenly it hurled itself against a house. The men swore and Floralie blushed because she had heard forbidden words. The carriage struck the horse, or a tree, like an enormous whip. Windows shattered and a wheel was always flung out into the middle of the road, slicing like a knife at first, then slowing down, hesitating, until eventually it flattened out against a wall. But the horse was still fleeing. It might leave the village to lose itself in the forest or, running away, it might strangle in its harness. Then a man detached himself from a group. The others were quiet; the old women murmured "Jesus." He moved along the road, his arms open so that the horse would understand that it would not be allowed to pass. The horse charged the man, rearing up and threatening him with its forefeet. The man slipped past, seized the bridle and pulled with all his might, tearing at the horse's mouth. The horse, whinnying, dragged the man along and little by little relented, giving in to the man at last. It stopped, glistening with sweat and panting. The man would put his hand in the horse's mane, patting the collar so the horse would know that it was forgiven. The men and children

8

could approach and the women would beg them to be careful.

Once the horse had lunged at a man and trampled him. The man was supposed to get married the next day and the horse was the one he had rented for the wedding.

The mane of the horse that had brought the young man down was as furious as that of Anthyme's horse.

Anthyme controlled the horse very well, but Floralie was still afraid.

*   *   *

Suddenly Anthyme pulled on the reins so hard that the horse's head was turned around. Its jaw, tortured by the bit, seemed like an open wound. The animal tried to resist. It reared up and tried to turn its head back into place. Anthyme, with another short pull on the reins, reminded him who was boss. The horse gave in, quietly. Anthyme released the reins. The head, then the collar, sank slowly towards the ground and the animal licked at the grass, seeking a little freshness. There was no sound from the motionless wheels. The earth no longer resounded under the hooves and the buggy stopped complaining. No sound could be heard except the horse's breathing. The whole forest, the whole earth seemed to be breathing through its lumgs. The trees were frozen in their silence. Despite the sweat, everything that Floralie saw seemed to be fixed in an invisible ice. She shivered in her thin black gown. The trip had tired her out, and it had barely begun. The buggy, jolting at too lively a pace, had shaken her so much that all her thoughts were in disarray. She could not even think. Even

9

though the vehicle had stopped she felt as if the wheels were still turning over the bumps and potholes, as if the ground were trembling beneath her. She could think of nothing but that sensation. Although she could see the horse, crestfallen, its legs weak, its head hanging above the grass, rubbing its nose among the leaves, it really seemed as if it were still running.

Anthyme, seated, listened to his own breathing for a moment, saying nothing. With elaborate care he tied the reins to the apron of the buggy, then suddenly he jumped to the ground.

"Get down," he said.

She got down. When you marry a man you follow him and obey him. During the first weeks she would have to repeat to herself that women are made to obey; then, as she got used to it, she would obey without even thinking about it.

"Come with me," he ordered.

She followed him, her short steps following his long ones as he sank into the ferns. She stopped to put her finger on a touch-me-not, the tiny flower so bright and fragile in the shade.

"Are you coming?"

He knew where he was taking her. Under a very old spruce covered with grey moss, its branches spread out to form a roof, Anthyme turned towards Floralie.

"It's pretty here."

The spruce was redolent of all the freshness that had perfumed the Decembers of his childhood. The fallen needles formed a soft carpet.

"It's pretty," Floralie repeated.

"We'll be nice and comfortable."

"When we were little we used to make houses under the pine trees."

"This is a spruce."

"It's a tree."

"Now you're going to really be my wife."

He took off his jacket, spread it over the carpet of needles and pulled off his necktie. As he unbuttoned his shirt Floralie could see his white shoulders and hairy chest. She watched, saying nothing. Anthyme looked her up and down.

"What's the matter? Have you turned into a pillar of salt?"

A tear pricked at her eyelid, but she dared not move her hand to wipe it away. Such a gesture seemed to be forbidden by some strict law.

"Don't cry, *hostie!* This is the happiest day of your life."

Anthyme let down his trousers and, keeping his shoes on, freed first one leg, then the other. He put on his best smile. Then, the lower part of his body enclosed in long woollen underpants like Floralie had seen on her father, he came up to her, smelling strongly of horse.

"Floralie," he pleaded, "take off your dress. You know very well we can't do it with all our clothes on."

She realized how small she was in front of this man who was her husband. Her legs were pressed tightly together and her arms were crossed on her bosom. She would move only if she were forced.

"What's the matter?"

"I've got a stomach ache."

"I don't believe you. *Hostie!* We haven't made a baby yet."

"I ate too much molasses pie. I'll never be able to make them as good as my mother . . . so I wanted to eat as much as I could . . . "

He gathered her into his arms. Her ear stuck against his sweaty chest, Floralie could hear his heart galloping like a mad horse.

"Floralie . . . do you love me?"

"You're my husband, Anthyme."

He could hear only boredom in her voice.

"What's the matter with you? Are you my wife or aren't you?"

She did not reply. Anthyme expected a word at least.

"Anyway, I won't take off my underwear till you take off your dress."

He shaped his mouth, which had become sad, back into a smile.

"I can't wait to see you naked."

"Why?"

"Because you're my wife. And because I'm a man. And because the good Lord made men and women. And because the good Lord is perfect."

Anthyme had moved his hand from her shoulder down to her thigh in a reassuring caress, hoping to tame this nervous little animal that was his wife. She seemed to give in, to tolerate the hand which had become more insistent. Suddenly she disengaged herself, pushed Anthyme's hand away, stepped back a few paces and gave him a look in which he could feel her mistrust.

"As far as I'm concerned my eyes are staying shut. I don't want to see *you* naked."

If Floralie had been a man Anthyme would have replied with a fist in her face or a kick in her belly. That always paralyzes the enemy. But Floralie was a woman.

How did you reply to a woman? Perhaps a gentle answer would be best. He said, in his most tender voice, "Sometimes us men, we talk a lot, we talk loud. But we don't always know as much as we say we do. I want you to know I've never seen a naked woman."

"Not even your sisters?"

"When they were babies."

Anthyme seized his wife again and pressed himself against her. "It's not me that made men and women, *hostie,* it's the good Lord!"

His arms were knotted on her back. Floralie was surrounded by strong chains. Slowly, he bent his knees and let himself down to the ground without releasing his embrace. On the contrary, he tightened it, as though he were trying to drown Floralie in himself. She was silent. He had recovered his panting breath; his damp lips, circled by his coarse beard, covered Floralie's face.

"I'm going to get undressed because you want me to," she said finally.

Anthyme opened his arms and freed her. She brought her hands up to the high collar of her dress, unfastened the buttons, the long row of buttons, and slipped the dress off her shoulders. She emerged dazzling in silk and lace. She folded her dress, then looked for some grass to lay it on.

Anthyme looked at his wife with admiration. After a little resistance, which was quite understandable, she had given in to reason. It was a difficult moment.

"It's a moment a woman remembers: after birth and death, it's the most important moment of a woman's life. You can't remember being born, or dying either, probably, but a woman always remembers when she became a woman."

Floralie was submissive now. Under the petticoat that she lifted, the flesh of her thighs, her belly, her little breasts blossomed like a glorious flower. Anthyme had trouble keeping his eyes open. They were burning as if he had looked directly into the sun.

"Come on!" he said, patting the ground near him to indicate where he wanted her to sit.

She came like a good little dog. He started to take off his woollen drawers. Floralie stretched out on the carpet of dead needles that nibbled at her flesh.

Anthyme did not dare to touch her. Dazzled, he could not even brush this woman's flesh with his fingertip. He was afraid, like a person who doesn't dare touch a fascinating flame.

Floralie jumped to her feet, crying, "Anthyme, look!"

"Where?"

"There!"

She pointed towards the ground, but what could he see among the bushes and ferns in the undergrowth where everything was shaded in green?

"There, in the roots."

"*There,*" grumbled Anthyme, "I don't know where 'there' is."

He got up impatiently.

"A snake! Near that bump in the root. Can't you see it?"

"It's a tiny little garter snake. It can't hurt you."

"It's awful."

Floralie's face was crumpled with tears. "A garter snake is still a snake, and a snake is the devil."

Anthyme wanted to take her in his arms to pacify her. She pushed him away.

"It's a harmless little garter snake. The devil," he said teasing, "the devil has no business here. If we weren't married, sure; but are you my wife or aren't you? "

Floralie drew back to get away from the snake, which was rolled up, completely still. Its little tongue was flickering outside its mouth.

"It's looking at us!"

Anthyme advanced, avoiding the dead branches on the ground. He bent towards the creature, grabbed it by the tail and brought it up to the level of his eyes.

"It isn't the devil; it hasn't got any horns. It's a little green garter snake."

"You shouldn't have touched it."

Anthyme came out from under the branches. Still holding the snake by the tail he whirled it around and, with a great laugh that echoed through the forest, threw it over the top of the trees.

"See what I did with the devil?"

"You shouldn't have."

His wife's fear amused him. And because he was not afraid he felt strong, and proud to be a man.

"I'm so scared."

She was trembling. The more frightened she was the stronger he felt.

Suddenly Floralie grabbed up her clothes and raced away from their retreat.

*   *   *

Not laughing like lovers enjoying themselves, but terrified, her clothes in her hands, panic-stricken, Floralie ran towards the buggy, oblivious to the sharp weeds that grew in the perpetual shadows, ignoring the bushes that scratched at her legs. She jumped into the carriage, untied the reins and struck out desperately at the horse, which took its time about responding to this feminine anger. She struck with all the strength of her fear, but the animal was unmoved.

Anthyme caught up with her, snatched away the reins and without a word began to strike the horse as though he wanted to engrave the marks of his whip on the horse's back forever. The carriage was yanked off the ground, fell back and then began once again to fly over the bumps and hollows, twisting and creaking on the road that seemed as if it would never end.

At such a speed the horse ran the risk of stumbling over a stone and being crushed under the buggy, but Anthyme did not stop whipping. When he judged that the horse had been beaten enough that it would no longer risk its life by stopping, Anthyme tied the reins to the apron, enjoying the sight of the animal trembling with fear. He glanced towards Floralie. His wife's eyes were no longer shining with fear: they were grey with regret.

"She won't put up a fight now." A smile spread on his lower lip.

Floralie closed her eyes. Anthyme swept her up and held her tightly in his arms. He had trouble breathing now. He began to groan. His legs were crossed behind Floralie's and their two bodies rolled together. In the buggy, shaking as if it were tumbling down a rocky hillside, Floralie became Anthyme's wife. In silence.

*   *   *

The horse dragged them along for a long time. They didn't talk. On the rough planks of the buggy's floor they didn't move. They lay united, cleaving to one another. She was scarcely breathing, while Anthyme was panting like an exhausted horse. They let themselves drift as the buggy continued along the dips and hollows of the road. Floralie opened her eyes. The branches hovered above her like great black birds and the sky was turning like a silent wheel. The buggy's shaking became more subdued, slower. Gradually it came to a stop. Without a word Anthyme freed her from his embrace and got up.

"No!" she begged.

She hadn't wanted to say it. The cry had burst from the bottom of her heart as her husband looked at her — with blazing eyes that she had never seen in him, the eyes of a stranger. She hid her bosom with her hand. Anthyme jumped down from the carriage and, patting the horse's rump, said, "You're a good animal."

Floralie did up her dress.

*   *   *

Anthyme came back to her.

"Get down. We're going to take a rest."

He went to rummage around in the back of the buggy and took a red blanket out of their baggage.

"Come on, it'll be nice."

He looked for a little clearing in the tall grass and prickly bushes. Floralie watched him unfold the red blanket and spread it on the ground. He lay down.

"Come on!"

He pointed to a spot close to him. She obeyed and lay down on her back. The big hand unfastened her buttons one by one. As the dress opened her breasts burst out, sparkling in the light. The hand climbed onto her bosom and rested there.

Floralie was thinking of nothing. She was no longer afraid. The stone that had been at the bottom of her heart had become a butterfly coursing through her blood. Her worry had been extinguished like a little fire in the depths of the night. The sun was flooding the universe and if they had not been protected by the vault of the branches the light would have been blinding.

Floralie forgot Anthyme, forgot that she was his wife. She no longer remembered the bumpy road or the horse's blazing mane. She gave herself up to the simple joy of breathing, even forgetting to breathe just as the river forgets that time is flowing through it. She looked absentmindedly at the sky and no longer felt the earth beneath her body. The sky fled as the road had fled under the buggy-wheels, and farther away, beyond the sky, Floralie heard the music of distant wheels. She thought of a locomotive, but there are no locomotives behind the sky. From the depths of her memory the song of wheels on rails hammered more and more insistently. She heard them coming close, saw the smoke belching out, then she saw the locomotive itself, ready to burst with its power.

It was a day that time could never stain. The locomotive from far away had appeared in the field. Floralie was wearing her Sunday dress with its pink ribbons. For the rest of her life she would remember the frenzied people, the squealing children who doubted the train's existence until it actually arrived.

She would never forget the uproar, all through the spring and summer, of axes attacking the trees. When a tree was felled, with leafy murmurs and a dry crackling, axes sounded in the trunk to square it off. That spring and that summer had been more precious than all her childhood. She could think of no sound as beautiful as the sound of the axes in the wood, and of the steel mallets pounding in big nails. The wood from which the ties were made was young and the nails entered badly. The mallets trembled and stuck in the wood; the men swore and Floralie was afraid because they were so strong. She smiled at all the sounds singing in her memory.

Anthyme slept.

Some workers were boarding at her father's house: five or six to a room, in the beds, on the floor, head on a rolled-up pair of trousers that served as a pillow. Several slept in the barn too, to save the money they earned at their construction jobs. There were Italians who were always talking, stopping only when one of them brought out a knife. Then Floralie's mother would shout, "Floralie, I need you!" and the Italians would begin to laugh again. There were Poles too, who looked up at the sky as they listened to someone playing the accordion. And Ukrainians, with wide trousers, who were never happy. All of them used to work from the time the sun appeared over the horizon, stopping only when their eyes could no longer penetrate the shadows. All day long her mother prepared meals, sweating, gesticulating, jostling, complaining, trying to make herself understood with gestures. She stepped over the sleeping bodies on the floor, scolded those with mud on their feet, wakened the ones who had fallen asleep in a chair or with their heads on the table, waiting for their plates.

Finally it was the day for the train to arrive. Floralie had never seen a train. Everyone — the villagers, the Italians, the Poles, the Ukrainians, cousins from other villages — had come down into the valley. They seemed to get along well with each other; everyone spoke together; the women and young girls wearing their prettiest dresses and the men their Sunday suits — except for the immigrants, who had only their work clothes. Suddenly, like a long, drawn-out peal of thunder from behind the mountain, the train surged into view. It was black and it belched black smoke, and it was faster than any horse. It was hard to believe that it was a real train.

A man got up on someone's shoulders so that he was higher than the others, and began to shout.

"As the official candidate for the opposition in this county I wish to express my undying opposition to this engine, this locomotive, this train that is already strewing material and moral disorder across our peaceful countryside and which today is sowing seeds of sadness that we will harvest some day soon. With this train going off to the cities do you think our children are going to stay in the country with us? Let us unite in opposition to the passage of this train on our land where it is sowing despair. Its cars are filled with misery. As the poet said, 'Farther fields are not as green as some people say they are.' Let us stay at home. Ladies, gentlemen, dear voters, look at the cows run away. They're afraid of the train. A cow that's afraid doesn't give milk; without milk we won't be able to feed our little French Canadians. Without little French Canadians, no more Canada. Without Canada, no little French Canadians. And when there aren't any more little French Canadians, what are you going to do then? There won't be anything left but *maudits Anglais*."

Floralie remembered the man who had gesticulated with his raised fist. She heard again the music of the immigrants who greeted the train's arrival. Here and there among the crowd an accordion, a harmonica, a guitar and a violin began to play different tunes. Then gradually they united in the same song. Floralie would never forget their singing.

A young Italian who was staying at her place, a child almost, had come up to her. Soon his shoulder was grazing hers and a caress flashed through the young girl's body. He stretched his arm behind her, and his hand came to rest on her thigh. Floralie's legs trembled as though the ground had reverberated under her feet. She had never experienced such overpowering joy. He was handsome, with his black hair and his eyes that looked as though they were never in the wrong. She discovered the marvel of being alive, of having her blood maddened by a young man's look. The marvel of being a girl. When she was serving plates to the boarders between the tables in the dining room, from which the furniture had been removed, she often felt a hand on her bottom or an arm around her waist. Floralie pushed them away impatiently. She was afraid of virile hands, those five-footed beasts clambering over her. At the very moment when the train arrived in the valley, the Italian's arm, his hand nervous as a bird, changed her life. On that day a life began where nothing would ever again resemble what it had been before.

The labourers, the immigrants, the people from the village all ran towards the train and followed along after it. The train went on its way, making a mooing sound. Behind it men and women and children sang songs that made them laugh. Soon silence would return to the sleepy valley and the young Italian would go away to await the arrival of another train, somewhere else. Floralie would come back alone to see the train go by. Someday, perhaps, the Italian would be on the train, but she would never know.

Floralie began to walk with him, following. They climbed the hill. She let her head fall onto his shoulder. He spoke, but she didn't understand. She laughed. If she spoke he laughed too.

He let go of her waist and took her hand. She ran behind him in the oatfield, which was beautiful — brilliant, tall and thick. They plunged into it as if it were pure water, rolling against one another, embracing, their lips joined. It seemed to Floralie that they were very near the sun. They rolled, rolled together, and the sun rolled with them. Floralie's dress was open and the Italian was pressing his face against her breasts. He could not open his eyes, the sunlight was so blinding. Floralie thought she was drowning. She did not struggle. The young man pressed against her as though he wanted to mix his bones with Floralie's own. Suddenly a burning sensation tore at her belly. She yelled with pain. The young man's mouth blew vehemently against her ear. Then the valley became calm again, like gentle rain; they slept like tired children. When she woke up she smiled at him. The young man's eyes were sad. Her heart became calm. Floralie opened her mouth to cry out, with a voice that would fill the valley, "I love you! I love you! I love you!" but she saw Anthyme's face bending over her.

"How come you're smiling?"

"People don't always know why they're smiling."

"I don't like you smiling like that. I get the idea all you women do that. I don't like it."

Anthyme took his hand away from Floralie's bosom and turned his back to her.

She did up her dress.
She was shivering.

*   *   *

Anthyme stomped furiously through the pigweed. He
was overcome by the desire to break something. He
clutched at the branches of some bushes that were as sharp
as the blade of a knife, pulling with all his might. The bush
bent over, resisting, and Anthyme loosened his grip. The
bush straightened up quivering.

"There wasn't any blood. I didn't see a single little
drop of blood. That means it wasn't the first time she's had
a man. *Hostie!*"

He attacked a thin stem with two leaves, a future
maple, winding it around his hand. The muscles in his arm
contracted. He held his breath and the earth moved around
the stem. The roots came loose, the maple came out and
Anthyme waved it in the air like a precious trophy. He
went back to stretch out on the red blanket. Hands clasped
behind his neck, eyes questioning the blue of the sky, he
reflected.

"She can say whatever she wants, but there's one
thing I know for sure: there's a wall you have to break
through. Not a stone wall, but a wall, a wall you've got to
break through. I didn't find any wall. Maybe that means
there wasn't one there? It can't be. So it must mean that
somebody broke through the wall before me."

The ground was hard under his back; he turned over
on his stomach.

"There wasn't any wall and there wasn't any blood. So I'm not Floralie's first man."

The rough spots on the ground were digging into his ribs, so he lay on his side.

"I'm not even a man, because I didn't give her a smash in the face. But I'd like to hit her. Maybe there was some blood and I didn't see it. Then I'd be sorry I hit her. But I didn't feel any wall."

The red blanket was as unbearable as a carpet of thistles. He sat up.

"Sometimes there's things you can't see. As a matter of fact, blood's a liquid like water. Maybe I didn't see it. But blood's like *coloured* water. And it's a colour that you've damn well got to see. You can't miss it. So now I know for sure that Floralie's had other men before me. *Hostie!*"

He swelled up with hatred.

A furious ox no bigger than his heart was being hysterical in his chest. Anthyme didn't dare look at his wife. He would not be able to resist the pleasure of jumping on her, feet together, and crushing her.

"If I'd felt a curtain... but I didn't even feel a curtain! It's hard to know... a wall? Maybe people exaggerate when they talk about a wall. But apparently there's at least a curtain that you've got to tear. But there wasn't any wall and there wasn't any curtain. The window was wide open. *Hostie!* She's had some man before me. And if she's had one she could have had dozens!"

It was impossible to go on sitting down.

His bones were twisting in his body; he could feel them, like the beams in a house on a night when it was too cold. It was not really summer for him now. He was shaking. Anthyme stretched out on his back.

"Me, I think it could be that this curtain or wall they talk about's nothing but a fairy-tale. Floralie couldn't have had anybody before me. She's an honest woman, she's no sinner. This curtain you've got to tear is likely something they've invented to make fun of newlyweds. So if the curtain's some fairy-tale, Floralie wasn't thinking about anybody but me when I got hold of her to make her my wife. For all the bother she gave me thinking about it, she deserves to get beaten up. I'm not a real man if I haven't got the courage to hit her and make her forget all about these other men, and bust up the pictures of them she's carrying around in her head. It's the good Lord that gave women this curtain. So if somebody gets her curtain torn by anybody but her husband she's a sinner. In the Bible they stoned sinners and Christ threw the first stone himself. But how can I tell if she's a sinner? I'm going to go and see the priest. He'll know if women have a wall or a curtain . . ."

The same thoughts kept coming back, tenacious as a saw that sank, grinding, into his head, his flesh, right down to the marrow of his bones.

"When I wanted to take her, make her my wife, show her I was her husband, she was pale. Didn't say a word. She was scared out of her wits because she thought I was going to find out her awful, shameful secret. She was scared I'd hit her when I found out about her sins. Then she started to smile and laugh and show all her teeth. She was glad I didn't notice she'd had other men before me."

Anthyme got up.

"She just kept quiet and me, I loved her, and I thought there's nothing as good as loving a woman. I was a little bit sad when I was thinking about all the years when I hadn't loved a woman and there she was comparing me to some other man! I was heavier on her than one of them, or I breathed louder in her ear than somebody else. She was making fun of me by keeping quiet. *Hostie! Tabernacle! Christ!*"

He swore without thinking about it. The words burst from the depths of his being, propelled by an enormous wrath.

The sky was inaccessible to his fist.

With all the weight of an unforgiving man he pounced on Floralie and hit her in the face. Then he buried his big fingers, like the teeth of a fork, in her face and shook her head as if he wanted to smash it on the ground.

"Whore!"

And the name-calling continued as he shook her.

"Anthyme!" Floralie begged.

"You've had every man in the parish!"

Holding Floralie's motionless body between his outspread knees, he struck her face, trying to tear away its mask of beauty and reveal the monster she really was.

"Anthyme!" she barely murmured his name as she turned her face away.

She thought she was shouting in a voice that could be heard far away, above the trees. And Anthyme's hand struck with much less force than he thought.

"Anthyme!" she said voicelessly. "My husband."

She raised both hands and her fingers brushed at her delirious face.

Blood was flowing on Floralie's lip. Anthyme grew calmer. He looked at the blood and smiled. He was overcome by a great feeling of peace. He loved his wife in spite of everything. He leaned over and touched his lips to her forehead. There was no woman he could have loved except Floralie. Since God created the world there had been a law which established that Floralie and Anthyme were created for one another, like the light for the day. He stretched out on her, placed his arms under her body (it was so light) and took her a second time. Inside her he found gentle fire, a fire with the softness of her hair.

He would have liked to go to sleep on Floralie's silky body, his face lost in her hair, but he was unable to accept the fact that other men before him had loved Floralie as he did.

He rose, dressed and spat on the ground.

"You're a fallen woman!"

He went away:

"You'll be damned!"

*   *   *

Never again, as long as she lived, would Floralie say "I love you."

She did up her rumpled dress and touched the blood on her lip.

The sky was beautiful, smooth above the black trees, with foamy clouds like the ones in holy pictures. Perhaps there were archangels flying among them.

"Fallen woman!" a coarse voice repeated from the other side of the trees. "You'll be damned."

Floralie was damned, but she was alive. She was young, beautiful. She was damned, but she was smiling. Among the tangled branches a ray of sunlight broke through the shadow and spread itself out on the red blanket. Floralie moved, to offer her face to the sun. She opened her arms and surrendered to the caress of the light.

She was damned. The sun breathed so gently. And it did not know that she was damned. In Hell, at the centre of the earth, underneath her body, another sun was blazing. It was not a caressing sun, but one that tore and devoured with jaws of raging flames, flames that killed like poisonous snakes. It was the sun of Hell that never sets, that is never hidden by rain, a sun of ravenous flames that gives off not light but shadow, stinking night, eternal shade. But Floralie was alive.

"You'll be damned! Damned!" she heard, as though her husband were very close.

The damned are not alive, she reasoned, because the sun of Hell preserves death just as the sun in Heaven makes things live.

The sun of Hell was very deep in the earth, under her feet, but perhaps its grey viscous rays extended, dying, as far as the roots of the grass.

A man from her village had gone far away to work in a mine. His wife and fifteen children had never seen him again. The miners dug tunnels under the ground, many miles under the trees. They dug in the rock and made roads like the ones you make in the fields. The man from the village was digging when suddenly a beam of light shone up from under his pick and changed the rock into dust. And that dust crushed the tunnels, the iron cars, the miners. The man from the village had been touched by a ray of sunlight from Hell. Men had gotten too close to Hell.

Floralie would stay on the ground. She wanted to smile at the sun that was illuminating the sky and the forest, to marvel at her new life that was beginning that day, but a coarse voice that was no longer Anthyme's was repeating, "Damned! Damned!"

As long as she could see the sun in Heaven light up the earth, as long as she could see the earth with its beautiful colours, like new dresses, Floralie was not afraid of that other sun, the fire of the Devil. The infernal sun was much farther away from her than the heavenly one.

But just as the heavenly sun kissed her body there in the clearing, so the other sun would take hold of her one day. Its rays would come to lick her body, so pale in its coffin. She would feel its bite. When someone touched her brow he would feel only the cold of death and no one except Floralie would know that the sun of Hell was devouring her already, each of its rays like a huge famished worm.

And Floralie's body, because of all her faults, would burn on the inside and invisible demons would come to dance in the walls of the house. Their claws would be heard scratching on the wood. Through the cracks in the walls and the ceiling they would laugh at the sight of Floralie's body as it burned. Their shadowy faces would be seen stuck to the windows and then slipping away because Floralie would burn in the infernal flames, as big as a sun. She would be consumed without smoke or ashes, consumed like a rotting fruit. No complaint, no tear would burst from her mouth, but in Hell her soul would shout, all at once, all the prayers and blasphemies it had learned on earth, spitting each word from her mouth like hot coals. Her soul would have the same mouth as her body, burned to a cinder under her white skin. Because she had sinned with her body her soul would spit out everything she knew of the world, everything she believed about Heaven, and when she no longer knew anything her soul would be nothing but a flaming, suffering rag that would not remember that it had once been a young girl. It would even forget its sin.

The forest was perfumed. Every tree had a good smell, like a flower that you bring up to your nose. The gentleness of the sun seemed eternal. Floralie was alive. Birds were singing in the branches, wild as schoolchildren, knowing nothing of the Hell that was under the earth, under Floralie's feet.

The Italian had left the same day the train arrived. Farther away another railroad was waiting to be built, a forest to be torn down, ties to be laid one after another like beads on a rosary. And all he knew how to do was build railways and play the harmonica. He also knew how to give happiness. He never came back.

"You shouldn't let yourself get attached to birds," said Floralie's mother, "because they don't get attached to you."

Would he have come back? Perhaps Floralie would eventually have chosen a local man instead, one who spoke the same French as she did, who heard the same masses as she, one who had learned the same things in school and seen the same people living and dying. But she would never forget the young Italian. Thanks to him her youth would not go up in smoke.

"Anthyme! Where are you?"

Behind the gently sloping branches the sky was a soft blue. It was the same sky Floralie had seen on the day she gave herself to the Italian. Afterwards the sky had been even more beautiful, above the tall oats that looked like an avalanche of pearls that had fallen on the young couple. She closed her eyes but the sky penetrated her, perfumed with blue. Floralie stretched out on the red blanket; the goodness of the sky mixed with the light had eased the little pains that were cutting at her face. The blood had dried under her nose.

"Anthyme, I forgive you for hitting me."

She said this without thinking, just as the sky was blue without any reflecting.

One day this whole forest would disappear. The road would be covered by overturned earth and torn-up roots; the villages too would disappear into the depths of the earth like a pebble flung into water. Heaven and Hell would collide and shatter like fragile plates. Then there would be the kingdom of night, the kingdom of Hell.

Anthyme had hit her, but if he wasn't a brute he wouldn't be a man. She called him.

"My husband!"

All the branches of the forest were mute. Nothing moved. She held her breath.

"Anthyme! I'm here!"

A sudden shadow, like a scythe, seemed to tilt the forest, which fell down on her. Floralie was alone and in the depths of her soul a coarse voice, Anthyme's, furious and desperate, was saying, "Damned woman!"

She was one of the slaves of Hell. No one could do anything for her now. She had been abandoned and there was nothing to protect her against the whips of remorse. Floralie was abandoned in the forest: every tree concealed demons, every corner of the shadow might be a doorway to Hell. The silence of the forest was no longer a terrestrial silence, where you can still hear the heartbeat of life. If a branch moved, a demon was climbing on it. The sun darkened. She was cold, so she went back to the red blanket, wrapping it around her like a cloak. Hell fire touched her heart; it burned. To keep her from getting away, needles from the underbrush clung to her dress, and their thousand claws held her back.

"Anthyme!"

She saw the Italian smile with his white teeth. He had long teeth and he was always laughing. The other immigrants didn't laugh like that, and neither did the men from the village. When the men were brawling, breaking wooden chairs, he kept laughing; and he laughed when a knife blade gleamed in the hand of an angry man. He laughed as he played his harmonica, and you would have thought that ten harmonicas were vibrating when he made his own sing. He danced with the vigour of a man with seven lives. Floralie saw him in his sweat-soaked shirt, laughing: men didn't laugh like that.

Might it not be the demon that had taken hold of Floralie's soul in the oatfield?

"Anthyme!"

*　　*　　*

Anthyme could not find his horse on the road. Many horseshoes had left their prints in the dried mud which was also marked by the passage of a number of wheels. He kept his eye on the freshest prints, which had probably been made by his horse. He saw some grass that had been trampled down by a wheel and several low branches that had been broken. Then the order of the forest and the road seemed undisturbed, as if the horse had flown away with the buggy. His horse was no bird.

"*Hostie d'hosties!* " he muttered between clenched teeth. He was dumbfounded by so much mystery. Nothing was moving in the foliage; light and shadow seemed made of wood.

Anthyme had thought that the fresh grass would keep his horse from straying off; but perhaps the creature wanted other things besides food. Anthyme should have tied him to a tree, but a man can't keep his mind on a horse and a woman at the same time. Perhaps a horse doesn't like his master to disappear into the underbrush with a woman; and perhaps the horse wanted to imitate his master and had gone off to look for a mare for himself. In that case, even if he had been tied up he would have taken off. There was no reason for Anthyme to blame himself for not tying up the horse. What had he done then to make the horse bolt off? A man whose own horse doesn't like him is no man.

"*Hostie d'hosties d'hosties!* Lose my horse on my wedding day! I'll remember this for the rest of my life."

Had the horse continued along the road? Had it turned back? Had it gone deeper into the forest? There were no recent tracks. No one had passed that way for days. Nothing had flattened the tall weeds. Anthyme, walking like someone who has a long way to go, plunged ahead on the bumpy road. He had decided to walk all the way to his village, to go home alone. He would blame himself for this day for the rest of his life.

"Lose your horse on your wedding day and then find out your wife's a fallen woman! No wall, no curtain . . . it was an open door. My wife was a fallen woman. And to punish her my horse packs up."

Anthyme speeded up, stretching his legs out. He did not want Floralie to catch up with him. Women cling like weeds: they're always right when it comes to dealing with a man, and the husband gets caught like a fly in a spiderweb. Anthyme was anxious to get so far away from his wife that she wouldn't be able to catch up with him.

"When a woman gives herself to somebody once, or often — I don't know which — she can't give herself to somebody else afterwards. She's only on loan. Me, I don't like borrowing like that. I don't like leftovers."

Now he was running as though he were being pursued. How he wanted his horse! The buggy would have taken him a long way. But he felt capable of running to the end of the earth, where the sky meets the earth, to get away from Floralie. Had he heard a voice? He stopped and held his breath, his feet riveted to the ground like roots. He listened. Nothing. He began to run again.

This was nothing new. Horses, quietly grazing, had been known to disappear while their masters' backs were turned. Suddenly, no more horse. No more horse. Vanished like a soap bubble. He had known people who had suffered this misfortune. Where *was* that horse? No one would ever know because such horses never come back. There was no reason for him to have such bad luck.

Horses had disappeared, taking their carriages with them, even taking a plough once, as if the earth had swallowed them up like a huge mouth. Such things had happened in his part of the country.

Anthyme knew some farmers, like himself, who knew a traveller who had been the victim of such an accident. He was a peddler who charged too much for the old clothes he sold to poor people. And he used to take unfair advantage of the women, too, when their husbands had been away in the forest for too long and they were dying for a man.

The Devil had come for the peddler and dragged him off to Hell, because the horse wasn't really a horse, it was the Devil disguised as a horse.

Some people thought it wasn't the Devil. Not the Devil? But its hooves had left black marks; they had burned the gravel on the road. The horse's shoes were red from the fires of Hell. That was a curse that had punished an honest-to-goodness sinner, a public sinner, but Anthyme hadn't committed such grave sins. He didn't deserve that kind of punishment: he got drunk only rarely, he never took the name of the Lord in vain and Floralie, his wife, was the first woman he had had.

Something else had happened during his childhood that people were still talking about. A horse-trader was coming back to his village somewhere behind the mountains. There was a woman with him whom he passed off as his wife, but in fact she was a girl who had run away from the hotel in Cranborne. The horse-trader and the girl he referred to as "my wife" were sitting in the carriage, the man whipping his horse to urge all the strength from its muscles. All of a sudden it was no longer a horse that he was striking but a flame as big as the horse; it was no longer a horse pulling the carriage but a blazing crackling whirlwind that set fire to the branches of the spruce trees, turning them into trees of fire. Even the carriage was no longer made of wood, but of fire. The horse-trader and the loose woman with him were carried off by the Devil in a carriage of fire. The horse-trader never stopped whipping, as though he was not aware of the flames around him, and the girl laughed with all her might because she was not really a girl at all but a demon in disguise. The fiery harness devoured a path through the forest and little by little the flames diminished, the horse began to fade away, then the carriage. The devil sank into the earth, taking the horse-trader and the fallen woman, still alive, into his Hell.

Where had Anthyme's horse hidden itself?

*　　*　　*

Night was coming down on the forest like the foot of some large animal crushing the day. Floralie was trembling among the upright sleeping trees. She had not stopped walking, the red blanket rolled under her arm. The night would be cold. Floralie would make a bed of ferns and roll up in the woollen blanket. When she called Anthyme, in a tiny begging voice, the whole forest repeated, "Anthyme! " but her husband did not answer. Why didn't he speak? Was it a game? Anthyme would spring out all of a sudden from behind a tree, fold her in his big arms, put his hands on her breast and rub his big, bearded man's face against her cheek. She was silent. She would not call again.

Her feet followed the path. She did not know where she was going, but a path always leads somewhere.

The sun sank slowly into the forest. In the distance the black branches seemed to be aflame, but aflame with a gentle fire that instead of burning slipped like rain, sparkling, down the length of the trees. The leaves and grass became grey, the dirt on the path became black. Her hands were so pale under the red blanket. As she walked the pebbles made a noise like little gnawing animals. How could she have walked in the forest without this path?

If Anthyme had been against her at that moment perhaps she would have said, "I love you."

*　　*　　*

Like tranquil masts the spruce trees sank deeper and

deeper into the night. Floralie's new shoes hurt her feet. Under the shadow, under the grass, in the rough spots and pebbles, the road seemed to take flight. When it was no longer visible Floralie would let herself fall and there in her red blanket, kneeling and praying to God, she would wait for the light to return.

The road faded from sight. She knelt and closed her eyes.

Suddenly there was a glorious burst of light. There were no more trees but, in their place, a golden field that was soft as a bed. From the end of the field, as silent as light itself, came joyful music, a tune she remembered: it was the Italian's harmonica.

Before her eyes, open again now, the night reappeared rooted solidly in the earth. The trees covered the earth like a vast night, their arms stretched out and their heads asleep in the sky.

Somebody really was playing the harmonica.

*　　*　　*

For a long time Anthyme had been running as if he thought he could escape the night, but now it had captured him, holding him in its claws. The spruce trees were closer together now, and their branches seemed thicker. You could no longer distinguish the road from the ground around it.

If he'd had his horse he could have been a good distance away by now. He could have been sleeping and dreaming between clean sheets. But he didn't have his horse. If he hadn't got married he wouldn't have lost his horse, and if he hadn't married a fallen woman he wouldn't be trudging alone through this forest where he was blinded by the night.

All his attention was concentrated on not straying off the road. Because men just as solid as him, just as strong, had not followed the paths, they had been forced to remain in the forest forever and lumberjacks had found their clean white skeletons in the green grass with flowers growing inside them. Other times the skeletons had fresh marks on them where wolves had gnawed at the bones.

Sometimes an old wheelmark appeared, then quickly disappeared again under the dark grass of the night, like a fish under water.

Anthyme had heard that a man can be swallowed up in swamps where the ferns, spruce and moss look very much like the kind that grow on solid earth.

"My one foot gets stuck in the mud; I move the other one ahead to pull out the first one and they both get stuck and then *I'm* stuck there like a tree. The mud is climbing up to my knees and I feel like a tree growing upside down — I'm growing down into the ground instead of up towards the sky. The earth can swallow a man the way a cat eats up a mouse. *Hostie!*"

Anthyme remained standing, his head raised towards the sky. He no longer had the courage to go on. It would be better to stay where he was, alive, than to go farther and drown in the earth or deposit a skeleton under the leaves.

The firmament was at his feet, rather than above his head. Anthyme wanted to plunge into the sky like a bird. Swaying on his feet, he closed his eyes.

"*Hostie!* I must be famished to be so crazy! "

38

He pulled up a handful of grass. It tasted good, fresh in his mouth. The forest was completely asleep; nothing seemed to be alive. The ground was solid under his heels.

A bird woke up on a branch somewhere and the whole forest was shaken by it. One minute it seemed to come tumbling down on top of him, then once again the spruce trees mingled with the night. Time passed among the trees like slightly stagnant water.

Anthyme would wait for the dawn without taking another step.

*　　*　　*

In the middle of the night, somebody really was playing the harmonica. The music couldn't be a dream. Floralie's eyes were wide open to the night as she listened and her heart was pounding. The harmonica's song was as real as when she used to take refuge in the girls' bedroom, throwing herself onto a bed the better to hear the Italian playing in the next room.

"Floralie! Have you finished washing all the plates?" her mother would ask every time.

Or Floralie would go to the window and imagine her life, and her eyes would close on the oatfields that stretched out so far, and Floralie would live inside her head.

"Floralie!" her mother insisted.

Someone really was playing the harmonica in the forest. Someone was playing behind her. She turned around. The music seemed so close that she shuddered as if she had been brushed by a wing. Tiny flying flames approached her now — eyes, perhaps — and then the harmonica music. And Floralie heard the noise of grinding wheels and the little sounds of crushed pebbles.

"Anthyme!" she cried out, happy.

Only the little flames trembling before her were not swallowed by the night.

"Anthyme doesn't know how to play the harmonica," she reasoned.

A horse she hadn't seen before neighed behind her, and its smell came to her face.

Afraid that the horse would step on her, Floralie threw herself off the road into the thicket, where her feet had trouble finding the ground. The animal didn't move. The carriage and the horse seemed to emanate from a yellowish spot of night. Vaguely lit by lanterns hooked onto the buggy, a man stood up. He was not alone. He addressed Floralie as though she were a crowd:

"Néron, son of Néron, son of the Almouchiquois, can talk to the moon and the sun. He knows the language of men too. Néron can find springs beneath the earth, awaken the rain, put suffering to sleep and stop toothaches. Néron makes women fertile, and also the fields. When Néron spreads his hands over a pain the forces of evil know they've been beaten. Néron, that's my name. Son of Néron. Have you got a cold? Drink the water that Néron has dipped in a holy bucket from under the ice of a stream at sunrise on Easter morning and bottled the following Good Friday at three o'clock in the afternoon. That water! I've sold barrels of it. Have you got rheumatism? Rub your joints with the skin of a frog that Néron has spit on three times while praying."

The man unfastened one of the lanterns and held it in front of him to see who he had been speaking to. The wavering motion brought the lantern close to his face, which seemed distinctly untouched by the night. His face looked like a bear's. On his head there was a feathered top hat. His hair hung down to his shoulders. Floralie felt his look weighing on her.

"Néron gives the love you've never had, and he gives back the love you've lost."

Children, hidden by the night, intoned:

Néron, Néron,
Is good
Néron, Néron
Is holy.
Néron, Néron
Is good
Néron is holy.

Néron added, in a supplicating cry, "O sun! O moon! O dead! Never cease to commune with Néron! "

He jumped down from the carriage and directed his steps towards Floralie, who was paralysed as though the night surrounding her were a black stone.

"Woman," he said, in a voice that was too tender, "tell me what causes you to suffer. Tell Néron your troubles."

The man's clothes could not be distinguished from the night. Only his face received a wan light from the lantern; it seemed to be unattached to a neck or a human body, but rather to fly like a bat. Floralie didn't have the strength to close her eyes, to keep from seeing any more.

"Woman of the forest, you need not speak; I can read what's in your soul. Your heart is a sterile land because your spirit wills it to be. The plant of love will never flower, because your heart says no to it. The plant of love is sick. Néron reads right through bodies. Give me your hands."

She made no movement; he seized her hands. Now a force was pulling at Floralie's hands as though her fingers were bound to the soil by roots.

"You know because I've told you, because Néron has said it — Néron, son of Néron. You know your soul is a desert and your heart is a stone."

She heard her mouth answer, "Yes."

"Néron can make barren lands fertile; he knows how to cure the pains of body and soul."

"Yes."

The two hands holding Floralie's fists were made of fire.

"Little daughter of the forest, do you want a river, a mighty river of love, to flow in your heart?"

Néron's lips moved soundlessly; it was Floralie who answered, "Yes."

Néron, Néron
Is good.
Néron, Néron
Is holy.
Néron, Néron
Is good
Néron is holy.

The refrain was raised again by the chorus of children, invisible in the night along with all the other little forest creatures.

"Close your eyes, little girl."

She obeyed. But she could still see him. What colour was his skin? Was it red? Yellow? Green? Were his long teeth black? Were they brown?

"Don't think about anything. Let the little voice deep down at the bottom of your head start to sing. Sing along with the voice in your head. That music is made by a river in the depths of the night, farther away than the moon, farther than the sun. Listen! the river is going to come right up to your soul. Your soul will drown in the river, so it can come to life again. Listen, child; listen to the song of the river that cradles and rocks you."

The river's voice grew stronger. Floralie saw the water whirling around like an eddy. The river's song became more and more strident as Néron danced around Floralie. The water was stirred up by a strong wind, a hurricane. The earth spun around Floralie the way it did when she danced too much. The water wrapped itself around her. It was useless to protect her ears with her hands: the music would have burst a stone wall. The ground gave way under her feet.

"Woman, the Dead Ancestors of Néron are dancing around us. They are speaking through my mouth and I am going to heal your soul."

The music subsided, the song became gentle, slow, long as passing time.

"Woman, pay attention to the flower of love springing up in your soul which is no longer arid like a desert. Look at the flower of love open its petals. Soon your entire soul will be blossoming with love."

"I see," murmured Floralie.

"You love! You love! You love!" Néron proclaimed. "O moon! O dead! O sun! You have helped Néron accomplish another miracle. You love! You love!"

Néron flung himself to his knees and seized Floralie's ankles, saying, "O dead!"

He slid his hands along her legs, her thighs, her hips, her belly.

"O moon!"

The hands moved slowly along her bosom, her shoulders, her neck, ears and hair.

"O sun! O dead! O moon! We have created a woman!"

Taking her, so light, in his arms, he went further into the night and laid her down on the damp moss.

Her sleep was illuminated by the vast light of a sky beneath which she kept saying, "I love you" to a young man with black hair whose name and language she did not know. The words were as clear as the oats and the sun had been on that day.

"Open your eyes," Néron ordered. "Come."

She followed the rounded back, the long glistening hair that was adorned on top with bird-feathers stuck into a ribbon. Near the carriage Néron raised his lantern in order to fasten it. By the light it shed Floralie recognized Anthyme's horse, his harness and his buggy. Néron took her by the waist, lifted her and, without effort, hoisted her into the buggy filled with quarrelling children.

"Sit down."

He got up beside her.

"My late relatives the Almouchiquois made me a present of this awful beast. I'm going to sell it."

With one crack of his whip he took command of the horse, just as Anthyme had done. The animal set off reluctantly.

Floralie turned around to smile at the children piled in behind her.

"We made you a nice Christmas tree!" one of them announced.

The others began to laugh, too enthusiastically. Floralie turned her head farther so that she could see better through the darkness where the reflections of the lantern's little yellow flames were meandering. A cry of fright was caught in her throat, for she could not believe the horror of what she was witnessing.

The Christmas tree was a little spruce from whose branches were suspended, upside down and attached by their tails, dozens of mice that squealed and waved their little paws.

Néron had seen too.

"What have you done, you monstrous little brats out of diverse mothers?"

Briskly he brought the handle of his whip down on the heap of children, who tried to escape the blows by hiding under one another.

"Lousy brats with your worthless mothers!"

As the blows increased, instead of crying the children laughed as though it were all a game. Néron's anger abated.

"You'll be sorry if you lose my sacred mice."

"We'll catch you some more," a little voice jeered at him.

"In the schools," another shrill little voice went on.

"In the churches!"

"Up the girls' behinds!" said another voice, less innocent.

The whip cracked through the air.

"Shut up, you fruits of sin! Put the mice back in the trunk where you got them. If you lose Néron's mice . . . "

"We'll catch you some more. Thousands! Millions!" one of the children assured him. "They're all over."

"In my mother's belly!"

"In the holy tabernacles!"

Néron stood up, whipped the horse, then turned back to the children.

"Stinking lousy brats! You haven't learned a thing about the beauties of the French language! I'll pound it into you in spite of yourselves."

Néron would never have whipped a recalcitrant horse with so much ardour. Fearless of the whip the children were jumping around in the buggy, which continued to roll along with all the strength the horse could muster. They jostled each other, choking with laughter. It was useless to hit them. Néron folded his arms. He had decided to use tenderness.

"If you let my mice loose," he implored, "how will Néron be able to sell mouse-skins for consumptives to rub against their chests? How will Néron be able to sell the mouse's eyes that you put under beds to find out their secrets?"

The children thought he was crying; not one of them was laughing now.

"Go on!" he ordered. "Put the mice back in the mouse-trunk. And don't let the frogs get out either!"

A little girl burst into tears.

"Papa, are you going to spoil my pretty Christmas tree? Why do you always ruin everything I make?"

"I can't refuse that one anything," Néron explained. "Is it because I love her or because I detest her?"

At the signal from the whip the horse picked up speed again and as it clattered and swayed along the bumpy road the carriage was a raft drifting through the night, with its three lanterns, the children piled around the Christmas tree, the trunks, Floralie with her eyes closed and Néron, who saw the road as though it were the middle of day.

Floralie's nerves were all on edge. She was so afraid that she would gladly have flung herself into the arms of this man who gave off a smell of muddy earth. She would have hidden her face in this man's chest, with his red or yellow skin; she would have put her forehead in his sticky hair. Fear took her voice away. In place of her lips she felt an icy ring. She couldn't jump from the buggy; her legs were too heavy. Néron put his arm around her and pressed her against him. She liked his warmth and she wanted to sleep.

The carriage jolted. Her head fell onto Néron's shoulder. She slept.

Behind them the children were singing around their Christmas tree, with its squealing decorations.

Néron, Néron
Is good.
Néron, Néron
Is holy.
Néron, Néron
Is good
Néron is holy.

In the forest, where night was taking root deep in the earth and spreading into the sky, the Indian declaimed,

"I am Néron, son of Néron, son of the Almouchiquois! O moon! O sun! O dead! Good people, give me your rheumatism and your phlegmy throats; give me your bellyaches and your troubles; give me your cut fingers and your broken legs. Women, give me your barren wombs. Give me your gangrenes and Néron will make flowers of life from them. O moon! O sun! O dead! Never abandon your Néron."

*   *   *

To Anthyme, night had always seemed as unreal as the azure sky. This evening it had swallowed up the earth and he was in the depths of night like a pebble at the bottom of the sea. He no longer recognized the ground; his feet no longer knew how to place themselves, on ground transformed by the night. The earth was as mysterious as the pelagic deeps. Just as Anthyme had never seen the sea, so he had never seen the night before tonight.

He had lost his horse, he had lost his wife, and the night was stripping away the very road beneath his boots. Nailed to the earth, he could go no further. He waited, his eyes on the sky. Dawn was far away, on the other side of day. All the small animals taking advantage of the night to come to life and crawl about made him afraid to lie down. Soon his fatigue would overcome his fear — then he would fall to the ground. Thinking, his eyes open to the night, made him dizzy.

Anthyme could have asked God, who never sleeps in Heaven, to hurry the daybreak and light the earth and the road in the forest, but God would never have turned on the sun for a man like Anthyme. He lowered his gaze: salvation would not come from Heaven. He fixed his eyes on the earth, which the night had turned into hardened mud.

All doubt had vanished. When he took Floralie, no little wall, no curtain had resisted him. Floralie was a fallen woman. Anthyme would have bet his right hand that his wife was nothing but a fallen woman, even though she looked like an honest one.

To wreck something, to give Floralie a thrashing, to beat his horse or smash his fist against a wall — that might

48

have relieved his mind. That kind of violence would have liberated his heart, which was crushed in a vise. But he was alone in the middle of the night. He could not hurt the forest, nor make the silence sob. He contented himself with taking several steps, but he noticed that he was getting off the road. He came back. He would wait for the light.

He was alone in the heart of the forest and night had blotted out his whole life. Nothing existed now in this insuperable shadow. Neither his village nor his horse nor his marriage nor his wife, nor the deception she had practised on him. Because of this night, Anthyme could believe that he had never lived the day that had brought him to this place. The night had changed that day into thick, black smoke.

There was a loud clinking of carriage wheels; someone was moving, cautiously. He saw eyes glowing. A spot. It was the blaze on his horse's forehead. His horse was coming back. He saw it as if it were broad daylight.

"It can't get along without me!"

Anthyme was sceptical of this state of dependency, but he was delighted to find a buggy that would serve as transportation. He leaped up to take hold of the horse's bridle, and with the other hand to stroke the animal's neck and reassure it, but he found nothing except the night. Before him there was nothing but night, bristling with trees. No horse.

He looked around for the horse he had seen — his horse — which was on neither side of the road. It wasn't ahead of him or behind him either. Could he have seen a horse when there wasn't a horse to be seen?

Anthyme kept still, upright, fixed, his arms pressed tightly to his sides as the night and the forest were pressed around him — a black snow, cold and soft, that was sucking him down. The night pushed at his arms, pressed on the back of his neck, crushed his heart. Anthyme could barely breathe. He was choking. The night was drifting into his lungs like dry dust. He saw branches beating like the wings of birds. Each branch was a bird with a huge wingspan, flapping wings that were tipped with claws. The branches were whirling in a black eddy where the sky was sinking like a stone. The sweat pouring from his forehead burned his eyes. The black birds, after they had wandered vainly through the sky, would strike at him with loud hisses.

"Christ! Christ!" he called. "Don't leave me here all alone. Come and help me. Come down from your cross or your Heaven or wherever you are. Come and help me!"

He thought he had shouted these words loud enough to tear through the night, but his mouth had been silent.

The black birds stopped tearing at him. He remained prostrate, his face in the damp grass, while the noise of the wings moved away. When he no longer heard anything he opened his eyes. Everything had returned to its place in the universe: branches were attached to tree-trunks, trees were planted in tranquil soil and the sky was very high above the forest. The night, already less dense, had begun to allow him a glimpse of the firmament.

A big cloud moving slowly caught his attention. It was gliding through the sky, with a sound like a buggy going along a bad road at full speed. The shape he had thought to be a cloud was, he could see now, his buggy, drawn by his horse. His own buggy; his own horse.

When you see a carriage flying through the sky it is a sign that you are going to die soon: the carriage comes to look for the soul of the person who has seen it. Anthyme collapsed, to melt into the earth. He did not want to die.

Life was stirring in his body, like a cat thrown into the river in a sack.

The buggy was no longer visible in the sky; it was approaching, coming towards him. The wheels were no longer rolling through the air, but along the road in the forest. The earth shook under the horse's hooves. The uproar of spinning wheels was shattering his eardrums. The buggy was destroying everything in its path. He tensed his muscles to make himself like a stone, but his whole body was trembling. The horse came to a stop. It was breathing down Anthyme's neck.

He should not have abandoned Floralie. It was the first time he had had a woman and he was no longer certain that he had not broken the little curtain that would prove she was an honest woman. To be fair, he should admit he had no proof that she had belonged to another man before him. Had he seen Floralie give herself to someone? And he, Anthyme, had he given Floralie any proof that he had never had a woman before her? After today he would never know anything as good as having a woman, but death was soon going to take him, capture his soul and carry him far from the earth in the buggy of death. His fingers clung to the earth he did not want to leave. It would take a lot of strength to drag away his soul, but who can conquer death when its carriage stops near you?

Anthyme fell asleep, the same warm sleep he had known on Floralie's body.

Suddenly an invisible hand grabbed his throat, another tore at his back, spreading his flesh as you would spread open a wall of bushes. His soul left him, abandoning his body to the wolves with cruel, mocking laughter. His head was as heavy as a sack of flour.

A voice that cut the night like a saw said, "Néron, son of Néron, son of the Almouchiquois, can find the sources of water, preserve the harvest from ants and frost, make hunchbacks straight, put out fires, fix broken bones, stop wounds from bleeding. Néron can read hearts and he can cure colds too."

The cord of the whip around Anthyme's throat was loosened and children's voices raised up a crystalline cry:

Néron, Néron
Is good.
Néron, Néron
Is holy.
Néron, Néron
Is good
Néron is holy.

"Néron can read secrets in onion skins. He knows when winter will begin. In the forest Néron knows which way is north and which way is south. If you're generous Néron will tell whoever is lost in the woods how to find his way."

Anthyme's eyes had begun to see again. He recognized Floralie sitting behind the man with the tall hat. She turned her head, hiding her face in the yellow shadow of the lanterns attached to the front of the buggy.

"I want my horse," said Anthyme.

The whip whistled above his head and knotted around his ankle.

He insisted. "I want my horse and I want it right now."

With a dry crack of the handle Néron flicked the whip back to himself. Anthyme's feet slid on the wet ground and he fell. The children, delighted at such a funny sight, twisted with laughter, applauded and danced.

Anthyme got up.

"I want my horse, *hostie!* My horse!"

The whip whistled and Anthyme felt something burn his cheek like an insect bite.

"Young man, Néron sees your heart and it's black, black, black as this night. Your heart is so black your blood is black too. The blood on your cheek is black."

Blood was flowing from the scratch. Anthyme put a finger to it and held it up to the lamplight. His blood was black.

"Young man, you're a coward. I can read it in your heart. You have a black heart, you have black blood and your heart is so black that if you made babies with a woman they'd have black skin. Your heart is so black it would be just as well if you never dared make babies at all. Néron gives you his word: they'll be niggers."

Anthyme was humiliated that Néron had succeeded in reading his mind so deeply. He was ashamed not to be able to look someone in the eye. He could live only by creeping and hiding like a snake.

"Your heart is so black even your horse refuses to recognize you."

"I always go to mass," he whined.

"Your heart is so black you obscure the night. What have you done that's so horrible? Néron will read your heart, and he'll know."

"I say my prayers three times a day and I don't even swear as often as that."

"Your heart is so rotten that when you talk a person would think he's standing beside a corpse. Why have you hurt another human being?"

"I don't love sin. I swear I don't love sin."

"You've committed a terrible sin because you've hurt a woman. I can read in your heart that you're not sorry."

The devil was breathing words into the ear of this man, who saw through every secret. Anthyme would rather have been facing a wolf.

"Come on, *hostie,* since you don't want to give me my horse I'm going to take my wife back."

Anthyme went towards the buggy. Floralie looked away.

"Come on, woman."

Néron said drily, "I won't let you take this woman even if you give me a horse in exchange. Your heart is so black you'd rape her and leave her under a tree."

"Woman, come here!"

"Giddyup! " Néron ordered the horse.

The whip clattered, this time on the horse, which had already set the buggy in motion. Every board was screaming at the violence of the takeoff.

Anthyme had been able to hold onto something that belonged to him — one of the lanterns, whose slender flame he brandished, shouting, *"Hostie d'hosties!"*

He wished his voice would shatter the night like a window: he wanted it to smash the trees and tear them up and hurt the sleeping animals. But the silence was deaf to his anger.

When the cries could no longer escape from his raw throat he threw the oil lamp as far as he could over the spruce trees, following the little flame with his eyes. It disappeared. He waited for the flame to burst out and smash the night, devouring the entire forest. He already regretted his action. His heart was truly black: it was the colour of a devastated forest where the blackened skeletons were dancing in the blue sky; it was as black as the earth where grass has been burned. Nothing exploded. The night remained black. The spruce trees were not turned into firebirds. The little flame in the lantern had gone out.

Anthyme was so happy he could have danced for joy.

Was his heart really as black as he had been told? The flame his hand had touched went out. This tree-filled night was like his heart: no light would penetrate it. He had refused to let Floralie's love enter it.

It had been good of God to keep him alive when his heart was so black.

"My God, who invented the light, I'm asking you not to squeeze my heart in your hand. My heart is so black it's possible you can't see what's in it, but that's no reason to punish me right away. Wait a while, God. Give me time to be converted. Then you can wipe me out."

From far away a choir of angels seemed to utter a celestial response to his prayer. But he soon recognized the words.

Néron, Néron
Is good.
Néron, Néron
Is holy.
Néron, Néron
Is good
Néron is holy

"When you've got a black heart it doesn't matter much where you go. You always take your black heart with you. I've been too wicked with my wife. Maybe she's an honest woman. I don't love sin. If I've got a black heart maybe I love sin. Or maye it's sin that loves me."

On that night, when the face of the man seated close to her was as unknown, as removed from her as the moon, Floralie was sound asleep.

Néron briskly tightened the reins. The horse stopped as it felt the tearing in its mouth and Floralie was almost thrown out of the buggy.

"You see what's down there?" asked Néron.

"Where?" murmured Floralie, her eyes still full of sleep.

Néron pointed.

"There, in front of us. On the other side of the trees, the other side of the forest. Where the road stops there's another road that leads into town. At the end of that road is the United States. Look. There. That's the United States. You see?"

"All I can see is the night. Everywhere."

"Your eyes are bad. Look at the smoke coming out of the factory chimneys. When that smoke comes down to earth it falls in a rain of gold."

"I don't see anything."

"Néron sees everything. Listen. What do you hear?"

"Nothing."

"Those are machines singing. They bite into metal and spit out chunks of gold."

"I can't hear a thing."

"Come on, little forest girl, let's go to the United States."

"Let's go to the United States," a chorus of clear children's voices repeated.

"I don't see anything and I don't hear anything," Floralie insisted, her voice pleading.

"Woman, you've got blind eyes and deaf ears. I've read in your heart that you like gold. Néron's taking you where the gold grows like wild strawberries."

"No! I want to stay here!"

"Here! What does 'here' mean? 'Here' just means wherever you happen to be. When the gold comes raining down on us we'll say, 'Here it's raining gold.' "

"I want to get out of here."

"No. Néron knows that you like gold, even if you aren't acquainted with this marvel. You're poorer than one of my little mice and you like gold. I'm going to have a white hat and a gold watch and I'll buy you anything you want."

"Let's go to the United States!" insisted the children. "Giddyup horsey!"

Painfully, the carriage was pulled out of the mud where it had stuck.

"Stop!" Floralie ordered.

Néron did not hear. In his mind gold was falling like a musical shower. Floralie, standing, was about to jump from the buggy.

"Stop! Stop!" she pleaded.

Néron had heard, but the rain of gold was singing louder and louder in his head. He had made up his mind to go to the land where the golden song would be wafted to him on the wind. He would have liked Floralie to come too, but she refused to go to the United States with him.

"When Néron works his wonders women kneel before him. They don't refuse him anything."

"Stop!"

Néron wouldn't stop her, this idiotic girl who was afraid to go to the land of gold.

"Go on and get lost in the night."

Néron pushed her scornfully. Floralie tumbled into the thick woods, which lashed at her face. She got up, dazed, astonished that she was unharmed.

The children opened the mouse-trunks and began to throw the maddened little creatures at Floralie. Instead of giving in to his first angry instinct at seeing the children waste his sacred mice, Néron stopped the buggy and encouraged the children to go on pelting Floralie.

At first Floralie thought they were throwing clumps of mud which flattened as they struck her. She protected her face with her hands, but when the mice began to run over her shoulders, their dripping little noses in her neck, when they caught hold of her hair and scurried among the folds of her dress, she was so frightened she could not breathe. She thought she would die of fright.

The projectiles came less frequently and the night grew calm, closing around her like a wall that nothing could open. From the other side, growing farther away, came the words of a well-known song:

Néron, Néron
Is good.
Néron, Néron
Is holy.
Néron, Néron
Is good
Néron is holy.

The very ground was made of night. It gave way under Floralie's weight. She was the last woman on earth. Her village, the men whose faces she remembered, the young men and their dances in their Sunday suits, the strangers who had come to build the railway, the Italian and Anthyme, all had been swallowed up by the night as it murmured beneath the trees, crackling under the branches. Only Floralie had escaped being buried alive. Floralie and Néron with his children. Néron with his bulging eyes. Néron, that toad.

Néron had taken her in his toad arms. He had looked at her with his toad eyes. Had he pressed his toad mouth, full of sticky spit, against hers?

The night had even invaded her memory, where an innocent toad smile prevailed behind a veil of heavy shadow.

Her stomach heaved.

She did not dare to move on.

She was alone.

Every step beyond the ones she had already taken could make her lose her way.

Who had brought her here?

She was hungry.

The forest was sumptuously perfumed.

She was hungry.

A young girl couldn't eat grass.

At each step her leg stretched out or pulled back, but too far, and she tripped.

A little water would have quenched the fire in her belly.

Cautiously, Floralie put one foot ahead of the other, without seeing. The weight of her body pulled her ahead. She was moving like a stream whose shores were the endless night. Floralie was lost already in a black sea; perhaps the channel that guided her steps would lead her to Hell, because her soul was so laden with sin.

How could she think otherwise?

At her birth God had given Floralie a pure white robe that it was her duty to keep immaculate. Tonight it was all stained with sins. Floralie had succumbed to the sin in which a man takes off his clothes, the better to be like an animal. God's anger must be terrible at the sight of this creature of his whose robe was as dirty as an old rag.

Why had her mother made her wear a black dress for the trip? Did she know that her daughter was mourning the innocence of her soul?

The road led down to Hell. Behind the bushes the eyes of amused little demons were shining. In the damp holes beneath the shrubs viscous little creatures were salivating in the shadows. They were following Floralie. At the end they would return to Hell.

Flee!

Floralie was walking so slowly.

Flee!

Floralie stopped completely. That way she would never arrive at the gate of Hell.

*   *   *

Meanwhile, Anthyme was running downhill at a breathtaking speed, tripping on the overgrown path, running on his feet, his hands, stumbling over projecting roots, scraping his hands, catching on branches that were hemming him in on all sides.

He was no longer afraid.

It had been a mistake to remain standing, blind and angry. The village would not come to him. The village would not come on a buggy drawn by a horse: it would take too big a buggy and too many horses — immense horses, at least as big as the houses in the village, and that would have required stables so big the people in the village could not have built them because they could barely build normal-sized ones. The land was miserly; what it had most of to give was rocks, and horses like that would have devoured as much hay as a whole herd of cattle, and his cows — what was wrong with his cows, anyway? Why had they lost their appetite?

Anthyme hurried.

For the village to come to him a very wide road would have been needed, like the roads in the United States. The village would not come on its feet — it would take too many feet. So, on his own two feet, Anthyme set out for his village.

*   *   *

Suddenly there was a peal of thunder behind Floralie, and the air stirred against her back, disturbing the shadows. Floralie threw herself off the road. The ball of thunder stopped beside her, like a carriage, with a sound like that of wheels crushing pebbles into the earth.

"What kind of animal is that?" a voice inquired.

"At this hour, in the middle of the forest, it's probably only the devil wandering around."

"It's a woman, unfortunately."

Floralie raised her head, but she kept her eyes lowered. She dusted off her dress with exaggerated care in order to reassure herself.

"It's the devil disguised as a woman," said a feminine voice.

"If you want my opinion, I'd rather have a woman disguised as a devil than a devil dressed up like a woman."

"If all the devils are made like that one, I say, 'Open up, gates of Hell.' "

Hearty laughter streamed out of the long cart, which was pulled by two horses. A garland of lanterns with dancing flames hung around the cart, where Floralie could read, painted in big letters: THE SEVEN DEADLY SINS, and in smaller letters: A Dramatic Comedy.

"Hell," said one of the voices jokingly, "doesn't open its doors to just anybody. Anybody can go to Heaven, but Hell is choosy. It only welcomes the nobility."

"When he opens his mouth it gives me shivers up my back," said a woman.

"Get up here with us, beautiful," said the one who was holding the reins.

"THE SEVEN DEADLY SINS, what does that mean?" asked Floralie.

She heard sudden laughter, like the cawing of a flock of crows.

"If there were eight sins the eighth one would be innocence."

"Seven is enough. I wouldn't want eight. I can barely keep seven actors alive. The public isn't very generous."

"It doesn't pay us much for all our sweat," said a woman.

"Seven sins is enough for one man!" said an actress.

They laughed like children, with sinister voices.

"Get up here with us, beautiful."

A hand was stretched out to her, and another, and Floralie held on. She placed her foot on the spoke of a wheel and they hoisted her up, very lightly, into the cart.

"Innocence," mocked one of the actors, "there's no such thing. Innocence doesn't exist. In the purest spring water you find bugs as big as spiders. And apparently there are some that are even more disgusting that you can't see. If water isn't pure, a woman ... No, innocence is all a dream."

"Lust has spoken."

The man had read the truth in Floralie's body, as you can read a letter still in its envelope by holding it up to a candle. The man knew her as well as she knew herself. She hated him for it and assumed that he was horribly ugly there in the half-darkness.

"You'll be all right with us."

"It's the first time I've seen the Seven Deadly Sins in flesh and blood," she said.

"Let's go!" ordered the driver.

"Thank you for welcoming me."

"It wouldn't be Christian to let you walk when we have a cart."

"You're right! We'll find a way for her to repay the favour."

What did they mean? Their talk worried Floralie. What would they ask of her? They were quiet. What were they imagining in their silence?

"Anyway, I promise to help you if you ask me to do something honest."

In the cart Floralie could not distinguish the faces any better because of the trembling shadows they cast on one another.

"I've got a marvellous idea," announced Pride. "This child can play the Blessed Virgin. At the end of the performance she could crush the head of a paper serpent.

People like the show better if the devil loses out in the end."

"And they pay more!"

"I protest!" said Wrath. "It's a wild idea. How can you offer a part to a young girl you pick up in the forest? Does she know anything about the art of the theatre? No. Does she know how to declaim her lines and make the rhythms ring out? No. Does she know how to improvise? No. You offer her the part of the Blessed Virgin. Is she even a virgin? "

"Are you a virgin? "

Floralie lowered her eyes and did not reply, crushed by the heat of their looks directed at her, which could read the undeniable reply. She should have continued to wander, refused to get into the cart.

"Passing yourself off as the Blessed Virgin when you're not a virgin — wouldn't that be a sin?" asked Envy.

She could not talk to these people who were tormenting her and she could not get away. She began to cry.

"Look at that — and you want to give her a part. She doesn't even know how to unclench her teeth," grumbled Wrath. "Tell us. Are you a virgin? We've got to know."

Terrified, Floralie hid her face in her hands and closed her eyes. Her gesture did not blot out the night, gliding behind her back like an endless serpent.

All around her, hands had caught hold of the bottom of her dress and were gently lifting it, looking avidly, in a silence where anything could happen.

Floralie opened her eyes as she felt the cotton slipping against her thigh. She saw eyes like atrocious mouths looking at her. Her arms slid along her body, hesitantly at first, then holding onto the skirt with more certainty. But the skirt, pulled in every direction, continued to climb. Floralie stopped resisting.

"She'll make a dazzling Blessed Virgin."

"But how do we know if she *is* a virgin? We've got to find out. I don't want to blaspheme the Blessed Virgin by giving her the body of a girl with loose morals . . ."

"We can find out."

Floralie saw the compassionate eyes of Lust approach her face.

"Get out, all of you!" he ordered.

The actors emptied the cart. Only Floralie and Lust were left. The actor took her hands and pressed them lightly, caressing her palms with his fingertips. His caress spread like a star in Floralie's hand and through her whole body the tide of her blood was set in motion by the insistent softness. Floralie could not pull away from Lust's piercing eyes.

He knew everything about her; he knew all her faults — Floralie could read it in his eyes, which did not shine in the night but had become part of it. His eyes had seemed ugly because she had wanted them to be. They were beautiful. She was afraid that she would lose herself in them as she had gone astray in the night.

Lust gathered her into his arms. Floralie's knees gave way and she clung to him to avoid falling.

"No!" she protested. "No!"

"You shouldn't say no to life," he said gently.

Heads surrounded the cart.

"Tell them to go away!"

"Now you can't even look where you want to!" complained one of the actors.

Without relaxing his embrace, and without being

pushed away, Lust had stretched out on the floor of the cart.

"Floralie! Floralie!" cried a distant voice. "What are you doing? What are you *doing*?" cried her mother's voice. "Is that what we taught you?"

Her mother's voice came from as far away as childhood.

"Damned girl! Fallen woman!" came the distracted voice of Anthyme, who was not finding the road between the trees.

"Little fawn, little kitten, little nose, little mouth," whispered Lust, "little delight, little love."

He lay down against Floralie and his hand wandered deliciously in the hollows of the young woman's body.

"I'm not a wicked wolf," said Lust, "I'm a gentle little lamb that needs to be rocked like a tender little child."

A burning sensation zigzagged through her body like lightning and gave way to a calm and fragile dawn. Gradually a little sun rose in her. It spread out with immense petals which hid the earth. Her body was as vast as the vault of the sky. The sun had the taste of the most delicious fruit. Could Floralie's memory, at that instant, not remember?

"No! No!" she wept. "You're handsome but I don't want . . . No!"

"Sweet little animal."

"I beg you! No!"

She was a rabbit and a wolf had her by the stomach. Her hands and feet were moving desperately. But she did not want to scratch the young man or hurt him. His breath whispered past Floralie's shoulder and reached her heart.

She could no longer cry.

66

"You're handsome, but we mustn't."

Lust drew back his face and smiled.

"I might already have a child in my belly. If you're the devil he'll be born with big pointed ears and only one eye."

"And his body all covered with hair," mocked the actor.

"I can tell you really are the devil," she cried in a voice that was calling for help.

She began to fight again, biting, frantic. She could see only her tears.

"Is she a virgin?" asked a curious voice.

"Yes!" Lust replied.

Around the motionless cart shadows clapped their hands, happy.

"Bravo!"

"We've got our Blessed Virgin!"

"She's a virgin, all right," Lust insisted.

These words wounded Floralie more than an insult. The actors, laughing, got back into the cart.

"We'll put on a beautiful show!"

"The public will throw beautiful money!"

"Thank you, Blessed Virgin."

"I won't have to rob henhouses any more!"

"At least not so often."

"Thank you, Virgin Mary."

"When we've got together enough money we'll paint on the cart, THE SEVEN DEADLY SINS AND THE BLESSED VIRGIN – A Dramatic Comedy."

"We're late. Let's go."

*   *   *

When he moved ahead Anthyme felt as if he was staying in the same place, as if the earth was sticking to his feet, as if the very trees were following him like dogs and he could not escape.

"The good Lord makes men and the good Lord makes women. The good Lord made women for men and men for women. Men expect to be ready, they look around, they choose a woman. This woman follows her man: she's going to help him live his life. A man wants to clear out a bit of land in the forest: he cuts the trees, burns the branches, pulls up the stumps and goes back home all dirty with pine gum and ashes and sweat. He has lots of kids. Every fall the barn is as full as an egg and there's a new baby in the house. The years are full. The kids wait for him in the evening. And the man, he finds the day too long because he's anxious to see his kids, especially the smallest ones, but the day is too short too because the sun always sets on unfinished work. When he comes in the house smells of baking bread. There's a smell of milk, too, and fresh laundry. Through the window you can see the wheat growing and you grow taller along with it. The woman is happy and as soon as the children have stopped tossing around under their sheets the man and his wife go happily up to their room where the bed is as good as Heaven.

"Maybe I was Floralie's first man. If I'd had other girls I would have known if Floralie was like them or different. I must be right: the husband has to break through a wall, a little wall that resists him. And I didn't notice any wall. So there wasn't one. Maybe I was too nervous too. If Floralie is a fallen woman, when she looks

68

at me she doesn't look like one. She looks like a young calf that's never seen the world. I didn't behave like a man: I behaved like a goddamn animal. I love Floralie."

He shouted, "I love you Floralie! I've been crazy! Out of my mind! Like an animal!"

Anthyme deserved to be punished. He would have accepted being sentenced to wander among the black trees for the rest of his days.

"Floralie, I love you! Why didn't you tell me I was the first man you'd given yourself to? You didn't say a thing. You kept your mouth shut — and me, I was practically yelling out loud because I was so happy to be loving you. And then when I got mad you didn't answer. Was I telling the truth? Are you a fallen woman? Are you as open to the public as a street? The street's public, the school's public, even the church is public, but I don't want my wife to be public property. But maybe you aren't. Floralie, I love you. I wanted to spend my whole life with you. I would have held you in my arms every night and then when we were old we would have spent the days rocking side by side in our rocking chairs. But you don't love me Floralie. And I love you! "

*   *   *

In the cart, which was creaking and groaning over every hole and every pebble and shaking up the passengers, who were a bit deafened by the blows resounding in their heads, the actors had made Floralie sit down and they had arranged themselves around her.

"I'm hungry," one of them complained.

"Some people only think about their bellies. That's where their brains are."

"Some people don't think about anything except applause. They'd slit their mothers' throats if it meant some applause at the end of the show," retorted the hungry one.

"Shut up! The main thing is for them to throw money on the stage."

"What's the good of money if you always have to work?"

Lust, absent from the argument, was contemplating Floralie's firm, round bosom. On his fingers the breath of memory sang.

"Listen," said Floralie.

"Listen to what?"

"You don't hear anything? It's coming from over there," Floralie pointed to the sky.

"It's the sound of a chain slipping through the sky like on the floor of a barn."

"You're right. I hear it too," said one of the actors.

"Me too."

"You're right. What is it?"

"It sounds like somebody pulling a chain across a wood floor."

"A big chain."

"It's the same sound. It sounds like a man walking in the sky with chains on his feet."

"And his hands."

"It's coming from the sky," Floralie insisted.

Talk became superfluous. They were silent. The horses pricked up their ears and stood still. The rumbling sounded like far-off thunder that didn't let up, but even more it sounded like a man wandering through the sky in chains.

"What is it?"

"Maybe it's a soul condemned to look eternally at the gate of Heaven without being able to enter."

"It's a sign from God," said the driver. "He doesn't talk any more, but he gives people signs."

The actors waited, in a suffocating silence. The sound was neither earthly nor human.

"God wants to remind us that sin is covered with chains," remarked the driver.

"The only chain I've got is on my watch," said Lust jokingly.

"Don't be blasphemous."

"You should be praying instead."

"I'm afraid," said Floralie.

They could feel the cold metal of the chains tightening around their wrists and ankles.

"The chains of sin are invisible."

"Let's pray," said Pride.

"Shut up," said the driver. "My animals are going to get scared. I don't want them to break all our equipment."

"Me, I'm just the way God created me, just the way he wanted me to be. It's impossible that I could be offending him."

"Blessed Virgin, pray for us," pleaded Pride, with the voice of a woman about to give way completely.

The others covered their ears. They wished they were deaf. Floralie got up.

"Our Father who art in Heaven, forgive us our trespasses as we forgive . . ."

As she was praying the sound of the chains became less insistent, as if each of Floralie's words were charming the clamorous serpents. The sky became a silent plain once more.

"It's a miracle!" shouted the driver. "I'm giving up the theatre and opening a place for pilgrimages."

"God obeyed you, Blessed Virgin. But I don't even know your real name. What is it?"

"Floralie."

"Floralie, the good Lord has obeyed you."

Floralie knew who it was who had answered her prayer. Because of her sins God had refused to hear her, but the Prince of Darkness, the King of Hell, where she would be going one day, had made haste to come to her aid. Were these unknown people who had picked her up really men and women? Or were they devils out of Hell come to gather her up in their cart?

The earth opened its monstrous jaw beneath the cart. The actors, laughing diabolically, and Floralie fell into the gulf, whirling around like dead leaves.

"She's fainted, the poor little . . ."

"Let's say the poor little saint."

"Our poor little apparition."

"Me, I'm going to confession as fast as I can. It's a sign from Heaven."

"What do you think, friends, should we make this a place for pilgrimages?"

"Me," bantered Lust, "I'm going to have to ask God to forgive me for trying to seduce his mother."

*   *   *

"Except for my little sisters," Anthyme grumbled, "I've never seen a girl naked. I've never tried to play the beast with two backs. I've wanted to often enough — I'm a man, after all. The bulls, the roosters, the stallion — they had the right to jump on the females and do it with them. But I didn't because I'm not an animal. I'm a man, I'm intelligent. Animals have instincts but not intelligence. A man has intelligence but no instincts. Sometimes you'd like to act like the animals, but you don't because you tell yourself you're intelligent. Many times when I've seen a girl I've wanted to rub her belly against mine, but the good Lord would have punished me for behaving like an animal obeying his instinct and not like an intelligent man. Then besides, I didn't get drunk that often. A few times a year, because I'm a man after all and a man likes to lose his head a few times a year, but not often. The good Lord doesn't like to see his creatures vomiting from drinking too much beer. I didn't get drunk as often as lots of other men. There are people who have drowned their minds in alcholol and never found them again. I didn't even get drunk on my wedding day. Anyway, it wasn't an ordinary day. Floralie was the first girl who was all mine. That's saying a lot. At least, that's what I thought till I found out that there's been as many boys on top of her as the LaFleur bridge. Then, before I took Floralie I waited for the priest to tell me officially to go ahead and do it. Not before, because I'm used to being an honest boy, but today, God Almighty how I wanted to be drunk — drunk as a pig, because a drunk pig wouldn't be scared like I am tonight. God in Heaven, blessed be your name, I'm scared. I'm scared the way I used to be at night when I was a kid. I used to have nightmares — wolves running around on the walls in our bedroom. I used to yell. Giants' claws would scratch on the ceiling and you could see the claw-marks in the morning. I cried till my throat was raw. Little red devils, all naked, with skin as red as blood, used to come and dance in front of the window. I'd call for help, but nobody heard. My brothers would never wake up so they wouldn't feel the hunger in their bellies and my father and mother slept like worn-out horses. I'd get up and go and lie down under the bed so I could cry. *Hostie d'hosties*, but I was scared. How can a child stay alive when he's so scared? My fingers and toes should be dead by now. A kid as scared as I was should have stopped growing. *Hostie!* I was scared! My parents' bed used to creak under their weight. That reassured me a little, but you, God, it would take more than a mountain to move *you*. You wouldn't have made your bed creak to reassure me a little. Where were you? Instead of sleeping all night like everybody else you were off chasing a boy who'd had some fun with a girl or you were knocking down some guy who'd had too much to drink. That's more fun than putting a child to sleep. Make a man suffer till he cracks up, then step on him. So where were you that night? *Hostie d'hosties!* I don't understand you any more than I understand Chinese. I just don't get it. I knelt down in front of your image every day of my life. I prayed to you. I honoured my father and mother even though I can't stand the old lady. I didn't blaspheme your name or the names of the priest's holy things except when I had to. Before I had a woman I waited to have her blessed by the priest. And to pay me back for all that you stick me with a dishonest woman, you take away my horse and you make the night come pouring down on me like a flood. I'll never understand. Why, God, why? I don't get it. When a man doesn't understand you shouldn't reproach him for what he says. Listen to me, God. I haven't got anything to drink. But if I did have some booze here I'd drink it right under your nose, I'd get drunk enough to split my guts and then I'd piss and I'd say you were right there in front of me and that I was pissing on your pant leg. I know, I know, God doesn't wear pants. You aren't listening to me, God? Other guys, the ones that used to jump on the neighbours' girls and laughed while they were doing it in the haystacks, the ones that used to go to meet the girls when they were going to milk the cows, the ones that used to go to Québec City every year and try out all the hotel beds with girls in them, one after another like my mother saying her 'Hail Marys,' all those guys have found little women that don't make eyes at men, not even their husbands. Those guys, their little wives give them a baby a year. They've got land and animals and houses that smell of fresh butter and healthy babies' diapers. But me — God — me, you throw a dishonest girl in my arms. Then you take my horse away. Then you throw me in the forest where it's as black as the inside of my mother's belly that I never should have left. How am I supposed to go back to the village without my horse or my wife? I could explain that my wife wanted to stay with her mother for a week and they'd believe me, the people in my village, but I could never make them understand why I'd lost my horse."

With tremendous strength, like the strength that comes out of the earth in spring into the trees and makes them burst out in buds, anger rose up in him. He raised his eyes to Heaven, looked for the spruce tree whose tip was stuck deepest into the sky, chose one and began to climb among its many branches, crawling up between the sharp needles, his arms tight around the gummy trunk. He soon reached the top, his face scratched, his flesh burning under his clothes. He could not hoist himself any higher, because the tip of the tree was as fragile as a feeble branch.

"God," he cried, "listen to me. I'm going to tell you something."

Clutching the tree with one hand he raised the other fist towards the sky.

"God, I'm telling you: you aren't fair! If you think I'm lying, come down and get me. We're going to settle this like men."

The night was stretched tight, ready to tear itself open. God held his breath. From the other side of the silence Anthyme could hear his own heart beating.

"You're hiding as if you weren't real!"

A drop of sweat ran down his forehead and blinded him. The whole universe seemed to sway under the weight of that drop of sweat. He held on tighter.

"I get it. I see what your little game is. You're afraid of a man who isn't afraid of you. Listen to me; I'm going to show you I'm not afraid. Listen to this: if I had a holy wafer and a hammer and a nail I'd nail that wafer right here to this tree and you wouldn't do a thing about it! . . . But I haven't got a hammer, and I haven't got a wafer and I haven't even got a nail."

Relieved, his soul appeased, Anthyme climbed back down the tree, almost happy.

"In other words, God, whether I pray to you or insult you, you're not the one that's going to feed my pigs or find my wife."

*   *   *

More than in any other place, potholes and hollows had torn up the road and thrown up pebbles. The cart was pitching violently in the tortuous ruts.

"One day," predicted one of them, "they'll shave this forest like a beard. The wolves will go farther away. They'll find rivers and plant grain and there'll be cows mooing among the women and children under the blessing of the church bell. Right here, under the cart maybe, there'll be a cemetery. People will think it's the gate to Heaven."

"When our cart comes back this way maybe we can put on a show in the village."

"If we aren't too old."

"My father only used to shave on Sundays," Floralie said suddenly.

The actors roared with laughter — she could not have announced the discovery of another America with more conviction.

Her father had a weekday face and a Sunday face. Today, for his daughter's wedding, he had on his Sunday face, but Floralie could only remember the one he wore all week. His hair was beginning to turn grey now; before, his head had been like a big black ball. Black hair, a black beard that hid his cheeks and chin, eyebrows like big black caterpillars, black eyes — and when he opened his mouth his teeth were black too.

For a long time neither Floralie's fingers nor her cheeks had caressed this black ball which, one day, had begun to cringe like a dog that has been beaten; but Floralie could remember how, as a small child, she used to play with this hairy ball that laughed or howled like a man in a rage. Floralie liked to remember how she would hold the black ball on her knees: she would amuse herself by looking for the ears and digging in them with her little fingers; she would comb the hair with an imaginary comb and with an imaginary razor she would cut the beard; it felt rough, like bark.

All of a sudden the black ball would turn the child upside down and crush her, rubbing her face, scratching her cheeks, crushing her nose, grating her ears, becoming hot as fire in her face. Floralie squirmed, complained, twisted to escape the weight of the fierce ball. She was so afraid — her face would be all scratched and bruised until it looked like a skinned knee. She called for her mother, crying, and the big black ball groaned with pleasure as it rolled on her and she sobbed.

"Stop it, Ernest," said her mother. "Can't you see the child's afraid? She's as white as a sheet."

Floralie no longer saw the black ball because her eyes were too full of tears. She only heard it.

"She's ungrateful, the miserable, ill-bred little brat! It gobbles up everything you've sweated to give it, and then you don't even get any thanks for it. You try to play with it and you don't get a word of thanks. You try to play with it for five minutes and it can't stand you. It sneers at you, it's already turning up its nose at its own father."

He was not talking now, he was yelling.

"If it didn't have a soul you could strangle it like a sick calf. But it's been baptised."

And he stamped his boot on the floor. The whole house trembled like the weeping child.

"You should step on it like a bug."

A caressing hand had wiped her eyes with an apron. Now Floralie could see her father, tall as a tree with his black beard and the hair that burst out of the opening in his shirt.

"I wonder why we don't squash them like bugs?"

Then, suddenly gentle, "Come and kiss me, little calf."

Arms were growing under the black ball, hands held out, waiting for the child.

"No, your beard is too prickly."

A scribbler lay on the table between the milk, the molasses and the cold beans.

"Come and give me a kiss or I'll tear up your scribbler and the teacher . . ."

"No, your beard hurts me."

."Come here and let me kiss you!"

"No!"

Without letting go of the scribbler in which she had traced her first words, the big hands moved apart and it seemed to Floralie that it was her flesh that was being torn.

The teacher had punished Floralie, who no longer had the courage to protest when the black beard ravaged her face. Gradually she learned not to suffer when the big black ball rolled on her with groans of delight. She waited with silent hatred for the end of the game.

One day her father completely stopped looking at her while she was in the house. She had not left home — she was still too young — but she seemed like one of those absent people who are never talked about. At least that was how she felt in front of her father. Had he even noticed her on her wedding day? While her mother . . .

"All forests and all beards should be shaved!" announced Floralie.

"The Blessed Virgin likes them beardless."

"Eunuchs!"

"Saint Joseph had a beard."

"But she was unfaithful to him."

"From now on my cheeks are going to be as smooth as the skin on your behind."

"That young girl will be pretty unhappy if she marries a farmer from her neck of the woods. They've got so much beard they could go without faces!"

"Get married! Go on! Young girls like her don't want a husband, they want a man."

"A husband's a man, isn't he?"

"A man sends his woman to seventh heaven; a husband sends her to look for his pipe."

"Sweet Jesus! Send us a bit of misery so we can cry. I've laughed too much!"

"Blessed Virgin, don't ever get married. You wouldn't have so much to laugh about then."

*   *   *

Ahead, the forest was growing light. An island of light animated the branches of the spruce trees but made the trunks more immobile, clutched in their strength.

"We're here, kids," said Néron. "Come on, come on, wake up. Sing! Come on, open your mouths! Sing!"

Like angels miraculously descending above the blessed clearing, the chorus of children intoned the hymn religiously.

Néron, Néron
Is good.
Néron, Néron
Is holy . . .

"More spirit, now. Louder! They'll be more apt to believe you."

From each side of the road, which was lit by flickering lanterns, there sprang up carriages and horses attached to trees, carts, wagons, horses with something to eat in their feedbags, children rolled up in blankets to sleep.

Dozens of buggies were lined up on both sides of the road between the trees, crushing the shrubs. Sometimes two or three horses were tied to the same tree, pushing each other with their muzzles and neighing. Others were sleeping and their open eyes were sparkling. Beams of light could be seen coming from tall pyramids of dry wood that were burning in the midst of the clearing. Some men were stroking their horses' foreheads, others were burrowing in the deepest shadows where only the gleam of the bottles at their mouths could be seen as the men emptied them with guilty gurgles. Women were rummaging in their bags, spreading sweaters and blankets over sleeping children. Older children, laughing, chased each other among the carriages, sneaked in among the horses' legs to surprise the drinkers and, with cries of delight, uncover the lovers. The girls hid their faces in their hands and their lovers pulled up their pants, grumbling, "You come on a pilgrimage and you don't even get a chance to say your prayers in peace."

With great uproar, Néron's retinue swooped down on the clearing, scattering the chattering groups and upsetting old men who were walking with difficulty. A cloud of dust surrounded the buggy, which stopped at a cry from Néron.

"Shut up, children; leave it to me."

He walked towards the back of the buggy. The children did not complain when his nail-studded heels came down on their piled-up toes and ankles. Standing erect, with theatrical gestures, he spoke to the people who were looking at the curious stranger.

"Come here, all of you! Everybody with pains, come to me! All of you with sore bodies, come; all of you with suffering souls, come! Come to Néron, son of Néron, son of the Almouchiquois. Néron knows so much about pain he can kill it just like you kill a fly by pulling off its legs one by one and then its wings and then its eyes and then its head."

Scornful and curious at the same time, the people approached him cautiously. From all directions lanterns were stirring up the night in an eddy of shadows.

"You over there with one leg, come here."

The cripple came up to Néron on his crutches. His face showed the strain of the effort, but his eyes were malicious.

"If you grow me another leg I'll say you're the good Lord and I'll install you in the tabernacle in the church."

Generous laughter exhorted the one-legged man to mock the stranger.

"With one single leg I've made twenty-three children for my wife, and they're all alive except for the five that are dead."

"You don't do that with legs!" teased a man smoking a pipe.

The other groups had broken up. Now there was only one group, gathered around Néron's buggy. The one-legged man went on:

"With two legs I'd have done twice as much: forty-six children, ten of them dead. That's a lot. Too much. The good Lord didn't want it, so he took back the leg he'd loaned me."

"Ladies and gentlemen, admire this man. Twenty-three living children and five dead ones. It's men like him who will save our country," Néron declaimed.

"I've only counted the children I've had with my wife Théodorina. I'm not talking about the others," the one-legged man remarked more precisely.

In their delight the rubber-necks frolicked like calves let loose in the spring grass.

The one-legged man's body was shaken by gasps and hiccups so severe that he began to cough, his face all puffy, his eyes bulging. He lost his balance and fell over, his crutch on top of him.

The laughter dried up in the farmers' throats.

"Move back, everybody," Néron ordered.

They pulled back. Néron jumped to the ground, knelt, and placed a hand on the unfortunate man's head.

"If he hadn't been lucky enough to meet Néron on the way this man would have stayed on his back pinned to the ground."

"That's a lie," shouted the one-legged man, getting up.

"It's a miracle!" shouted the chorus of children.

"I'm getting up because I want to," said the cripple. "That Indian is a liar."

"Néron is telling you: good people, don't pat a lion — you're liable to get clawed."

The country-people came still closer to Néron's buggy. The one-legged man went away, cursing.

"Since my eleventh was born," confessed a woman, "I've had a pain in my belly. It's like a toothache, but a really bad one that goes from my feet right up to my head and then stays in my forehead."

"Woman, give Néron your hand."

He leaned towards her, his head level with the woman's face, her eyes reluctant to tolerate Néron's sharp gaze.

"You're well already. Open your eyes and look into mine. You won't have any more pains tonight or tomorrow if you think of Néron, son of Néron, son of the Almouchiquois. You have been cured. If you want the pain to stay where it belongs and not come back, every Friday the good Lord grants you, at three o'clock, the hour of

Christ our brother's death, rub your belly with this water that was drawn at dawn on Easter Sunday. Here's a little bottle. It's free, but don't forget the widow's mite."

"Come, all you who suffer pain!"

Another woman spoke up.

"Me, I'm worn out like a horse that's been beaten too often. It's not my husband, I swear it isn't. He only beats me up when he's had too much to drink or when he's mad or bored. I don't remember a thing any more. I don't remember my sainted mother or my dead father or my happy childhood. I don't remember. It's as if I've never been alive."

"Well, woman, maybe you haven't," suggested Néron.

"I can't remember," said the woman.

"That doesn't matter. In God's Heaven the chosen ones don't remember their life on earth. Woman, you're already in Heaven. God has taken you into paradise before your death. Don't try to remember. That would be setting yourself against the will of God. Look, here's a button from the soutane of Brother Albertus who died in the odour of sanctity. Rub your temples with this button at sunset. It's free, because Néron doesn't work for money. Don't forget the widow's mite. All you who suffer, come!"

A young man held out his hand to Néron.

"Look at my hand, Indian. It's covered with warts. It looks like a rotten potato. Girls are as scared of my hand as if it was a skunk. Are you going to let me cut it off or are you going to take off the warts?"

"Give me your hand, young fellow. In three days your warts will be gone if you do as I say. Every day, at dawn, you put your hand in the first ray of sunlight and spit towards the four points of the compass. In the evening, when the sun goes down, put your hand in the last ray of sunlight and put your feet on the places where you spit in the morning. In three days, if you've really followed my instructions, you'll be able to say, 'Néron, son of Néron, son of the Almouchiquois, has cured me.' Don't forget to show your gratitude — a little something for the widow's mite. Néron relieves your pains."

A peasant with a muscular neck and broad shoulders stood before Néron.

"Indian, I've got a sickness in my heart. I'm a sad man. My soul is hidden under sadness, like a field under white November frost. I'm sad, sad . . ."

He was not going to say any more; sadness was stifling his voice.

"Speak up, poor man. Néron knows how to listen. So many words have passed my ears, I can understand everything."

"I'm sad," he repeated. "I don't know how to laugh. I'm a sad man. When other people laugh, I'm sad. When the sun comes up, I'm sad. When I've had a good day, I'm sad. I'm always sad. It's as if I've lost something, I don't know what, and I'm sure I'll never find it."

"Poor man, give me your hands — put them in mine."
The man obeyed.

"Néron will light the fire in you that will lick away the white frost that's covering your soul, and it will bring your sad soul back to life. Feel the fire burning within you, all over. The fire is beginning to dance inside you. Feel the fire in your soul. Your soul is waking up! It's stirring in you like a flame."

"Watch out! It's the fire of Hell!"

The people looked away from Néron, seeking the woman who had spoken.

"My good man," Néron went on, "I've restored the fire of life in you. To keep the fire alive, man, think of Néron three times a day. Don't forget the widow's mite."

"That man," Floralie cried accusingly, "is a liar, a charlatan, an exploiter, an adventurer, a highway robber, an abuser of girls and a wild Indian."

What woman dared to insult an Indian endowed with the magical powers of his race? Lanterns circled around her like crows. Who was she to accuse Néron? He pointed a threatening finger at her.

"Young woman, I know your soul and I know you're going under, body and soul, like a leaky boat. But the woman who gives her hand to Néron, who gives him her heart, is saved."

It was only too true that Floralie was shipwrecked, and that she felt as if the forest were the black sea-bottom. An extraordinary sadness caught in her throat, holding back the words. Néron had told the truth, and it was choking her.

"Young woman, Néron sees that your soul is as rotten as a little wildflower in the fall. But Néron can cure you."

He lowered his voice, bent towards her, and whispered in her ear something that the others thought was a magic formula.

"Are you coming to the States with Néron to look for gold?"

"Give up, you charlatan!"

Father Nombrillet untied the cord around his belly and, using it as a whip, jumped into the buggy. With impetuous conviction, he lashed out at the Indian.

"This isn't a carnival; it's the Feast of the Holy Thorn. Get out of here, you devil's sorcerer. I drive you hence, you money-changer! Liar! Thief!"

To get away from the storm of blows and abuse, Néron ran in front of his carriage and gave a command to his horse with a flick of his whip. The horse bolted into the crowd. When he had disappeared into the night you could hear,

Néron, Néron
Is good.
Néron, Néron
Is holy . . .

"My daughter," said Father Nombrillet to Floralie, "if your heart is sad I know the source of all happiness."

"Oh, yes, I'm sad, I'm so sad."

Father Nombrillet placed his hand on Floralie's brow.

"Sin makes you sad, my daughter."

Floralie wished she could come close to him and let her head drop onto his broad shoulder, but she dared not touch a man of God. The big eyes of this big man with the trembling cheeks knew a greater mystery than was hidden by the trees of the forest.

"Sin looks for joy, but it only finds sorrow."

"Yes," said Floralie, whose lips sealed too late to take back the word that escaped.

"Sadness is everywhere. It covers the earth because sin is everywhere. There are more sins than there are men and women; there are more sins than there are cows in the world; there are more sins than blades of grass; more sins than there are insects in all the grass in the world. Sin is vaster than the sea, and there's four times as much water as land. That means there are enough sins to drown the whole human race."

"Is that so?" she asked.

"Come, my child, so I can forgive your soul and your body, which has been a poor servant."

"Blessed Virgin!" someone called.

"Blessed Virgin? Where are you?"

Lust, all out of breath, took her hand, snatching her away from Father Nombrillet.

"Come, Blessed Virgin."

"Blessed Virgin!" repeated Father Nombrillet, incredulous yet respectful.

He genuflected and brought his hands together, dazzled, to thank God for the divine apparition.

"Blessed Virgin," explained the actor, "the Seven Deadly Sins have been looking everywhere for you. Where have you been?"

"The devil reigns over the world," moaned the pious man of God.

*   *   *

From all around the clearing, little lantern flames ran up and converged in a low flight near the actors' cart, which had been transformed into a stage by a wall made from a roll of muslin. On the part of the cloth which served as a curtain they had painted quotations from the Bible and religious drawings. On one side, the blonde curly heads of bodiless angels emerged from the clouds; on the other side, smiling out of the fierce red flames, were demons with red eyes and pointed ears, teeth and horns. At the bottom you could read, THE SEVEN DEADLY SINS.

The muslin was held up by upright posts arranged around the cart. Lanterns attached to these uprights by strings swayed as though the cart were in motion. The whole construction seemed very fragile to Floralie, as if the wind could tear it down.

"Blessed Virgin, why are you waiting to put on your white gown? There's one in the green trunk — it's got 'fairies, queens, spirits, angels' marked on it. You'll see it."

"I'm falling asleep," said one of the actors, yawning.

"Come on, hurry up! There's too many of them. I hope they aren't too poor."

"When the Blessed Virgin comes on they'll throw lots of money."

"Sssssh! Quiet! Clear the stage! But be quiet!"

The curtain opened on an actress wrapped in an enormous red tunic and wearing a sparkling crown. The people, with a murmur of wonder, raised their lanterns to see better, but arms blocked their view and there was an uproar of discontent. One by one the arms were lowered and everyone could see the woman, who dominated them all and who was looking at them with cold authority. If she had spread her arms she would have revealed the secret of her body concealed beneath the red tunic. But she was motionless as steel, inaccessible. The night, trembling in her face, made her majesty more fascinating. Soon the night belonged to this woman, waiting till silence had sealed their lips.

"We are the Seven Deadly Sins. We are the kings of the earth — we reign throughout the world. Listen, ladies and gentlemen. We are poor actors condemned to wander through the world without a roof over our heads or a place to stop when it rains or hails. Be generous today, this Feast Day of the Holy Thorn."

The queen disappeared. The stage was empty.

At the back a big brown ball had been drawn on the curtain — the earth; higher up a shining sun, with its golden rays; and higher still, above the sun, a hand burst through a white cloud, blessing, commanding or damning: the hand of God.

The people saw the woman in red return.

"I am Pride. Every man loves me more than he loves his wife."

In the crowd the women hoped that their husbands would press against them, reassuring them, but the men remained cold. The women despised their men.

"Even when they hate me," said the red queen, "they love me. The humble people particularly belong to me."

She drew back into the shadows as a fat man with a cigar approached. Rings gleamed on all his fingers and he laughed in his puffy cheeks.

"I am Avarice. If you are poor, you haven't followed my advice. If you are rich, you have listened to my advice and you are happy."

His silhouette disappeared, leaving the stage to a woman who came on languorously, her body swathed in a long, tight gown.

"I am Envy. Without me you would be obliged to accept life in all its unfairness, all its inequality. Thanks to me you can hate those whom life has preferred over you."

The actors were telling the truth. No one could have lived without the deadly sins. They secretly loved their deadly sins, but at evening prayers or at confession they had to say they were guilty of acting under their influence. Did they really regret having done so? According to the priests every sin was a gateway to Hell. You had to believe them. So they prayed to God for the gift of believing what the priests told them.

Two men followed Envy. They came on stage dancing, shoving, staggering, their bellies opulent. One was drinking avidly from a bottle, the other was hugging a pillow. They danced first on the left foot, then on the right and capered about as the farmers laughed, their shoulders shaking with delight. The two actors sang:

My name is Gluttony
No thin soup for me!
Sloth is my name
And sloth is my game!
We're both round and soft
As hams that you hang in the loft!

No one had ever seen such good actors. They put down their lanterns and clapped till their hands were sore.

"My name is Wrath," roared a man in a black suit, chasing the two actors who had preceded him. "It's thanks to me that life hasn't squashed you like common insects, impotent animals paralysed by fear, useless human garbage."

He had shouted his last words like insults. Without another look at the assembled crowd he went off, breaking his cane.

A pebble intended for him hit the sun on the backdrop instead.

A handsome young man wearing a lace jabot was already on stage.

"I don't say much, but I say it well. My name is Lust."

He reflected for a moment, then said, with a broad smile, "I am the father of all your children."

"You're a *baptême* of a liar," shouted an offended spectator. "When Mélina spreads her legs it's for me and nobody else!"

The laughter of the crowd did not trouble the actor. He carried on.

"I am also the father of all the children you don't have. I am Lust, the nicest of all the deadly sins. I live in your heads and in your hearts. You lend me your hands and your wives. I reign in your beds and your fields. It's through me that you'll be damned but I'm a very pleasant companion on the road to Hell."

Was he an actor? Was it the devil in flesh and blood there on the stage in front of all their eyes?

Before he had finished speaking the muslin at the back of the stage parted to reveal the Virgin in her white gown.

"I am the Virgin Mary," she said, opening her arms.

Sighs of adoration were raised throughout the crowd.

"You'd think it was a real apparition!"

"A real Blessed Virgin couldn't be any more beautiful!"

Women kneeled.

"I am the Blessed Virgin and I shall walk upon the heads of the deadly sins. I shall stamp them out just as my foot has already stamped on the head of the serpent."

Hand in hand, the Seven Deadly Sins crossed the stage, singing,

We are the happy
Deadly Sins!
We are the mighty
Deadly Sins!

We're the delightful
Deadly Sins!
Happy, mighty, delightful are we!

They went off laughing derisively, like children. The Blessed Virgin advanced towards the crowd.

"I shall stamp out those seven poisonous serpents."

Blessing, beseeching, Father Nombrillet elbowed his way through the crowd, knocking over the kneeling women. Leaping onto the cart he grabbed hold of the Blessed Virgin's hand.

"No, Blessed Virgin, you can't defeat the Seven Deadly Sins. They're stronger than you are."

His face was as sweaty as the face of a man working in the fields under the blazing sun. His breathing was that of a man in an indescribable rage.

"Satan is everywhere. Satan may even be stronger than God himself. Oh God, forgive me! But it seems, my Lord, that you are the weaker one. One could even say that your death on the Cross has not defeated Satan, because he reigns throughout the world. All Catholics should join together against the kingdom of the devil. You alone, my Lord, are our King. My brothers, listen to me. The Seven Deadly Sins are the Devil's army on earth. You can't fight them alone, Blessed Virgin, they'll ruin you. Come on, Blessed Virgin. These actors are the Devil among us. Take away their masks and you'll see the Devil's face. Get out of here, you strangers, get your cart off our land and go get lost. Clear out! Go prowl around somewhere else, you evil-minded wolves. And gorge yourselves on your own flesh!"

Beside himself, Father Nombrillet began to tear up the painted curtain, the earth, the sun, the hand of God.

"Actors, I won't bother damning you because you're damned already. By God himself."

No one in the crowd had the strength to remain standing. All were on their knees, praying, asking God that the Seven Deadly Sins would not try to seek revenge. Their anger was abominable and who could defend himself against the evil spell of the Devil in a rage?

"Go to the everlasting fires of the damned!"

"We're not going to get rich here," one of the actors interjected.

Father Nombrillet extended the protective wing of his arm around Floralie's shoulders.

"And you, little girl; I'm going to snatch you out of Satan's claws."

*　　*　　*

"Hostie d'hostie!" Anthyme swore. "At least I didn't get married in the winter. I'd really look smart in the middle of the night, out in the snow. I'd be dead by now."

As a matter of fact the May night was cool, but he was warm from having walked so long. His flesh shivered at the clammy touch of his sweat-soaked shirt. Fatigue had not yet put his muscles to sleep. The joints in his feet moved smoothly and since he had fallen into stride again, his feet moved solidly and without hesitation.

"At least it isn't winter, *hostie!* I wouldn't get out of this alive. And they'd never find my bones."

Around him branches disappeared under the snow and there were white spots floating everywhere in the night.

Under his feet the road was somewhere beneath the snow, running east and west, but the snow had obliterated east and west. It hardened under his steps. The white trees walked at the same pace as he. He was as hot as if it were the most torrid part of summer, but a cold wind drifted into his clothing. The cold was biting at his fingers. Soon wolves would come and devour his body. The sweat on his brow froze in his eyebrows and eyes. A misty ice separated him from the world. He hurried but he got no farther ahead. The snow was clinging to his legs, closing its jaws on his ankles. If he freed himself it would catch up with him at the next step. He stamped his feet and a big white cloud swallowed him up. The cold had warm breath and the snow was softer than the white sheets his mother used to pull over him at night. Anthyme fell asleep in the sheets of snow. His mother was leaning over him, telling him to sleep well; she pulled the white sheets, moved her lips towards his forehead — but it was Floralie's face that Anthyme saw.

"Maybe I was her first man, but the truth isn't written down anywhere . . . anyway, I don't know how to read."

It was a blessing from God that this was May and not winter. In December or January, by this time, he wouldn't have been afraid because his body would have been drier than dead wood.

Far away behind the trees Anthyme noticed, veiled at first by the branches, a burning that opened and closed like a red eye.

Soon the trees were long red columns mounting towards the sky. Would the fire spread from tree to tree and cross the forest like a bolt of lightning? He was sorry it wasn't winter, a winter so dead that nothing could set fire to it.

Anthyme ran into a cart without a horse, abandoned, or so he thought. Then he saw another. And horses tied to a spruce tree. And more horses, more carts, with blankets and boxes, sleeping children, buggies. He saw men feeding animals, people strolling about with lanterns in their hands. They were so indifferent to his presence that he did not dare ask what was going on.

"*Hostie!*" he remembered, from the depths of his tangled memory; "It's the Feast of the Holy Thorn!"

No more black trees sprang up in front of Anthyme; the ground was no longer muddy underfoot. He entered the clearing, where several fires gave off a quavering light. The people carried their lanterns and as they pursued the night it fled, resisting. In the midst of it all a swarm of lights came together. Anthyme headed into the people assembled in front of the cart and the actors. First he searched the crowd for familiar faces.

On the stage, Father Nombrillet was pursuing the actors, swinging his censer, and the Seven Deadly Sins were laughing, cavorting, teasing the priest; they sang.

"We are the happy vices . . ."

Exasperated, Father Nombrillet struck out. The crowd was mute with terror: these actors were devils in disguise, come to disrupt the Feast of the Holy Thorn. The priest, out of breath, sweated and swore; his censer, turning at the end of its chains, struck someone in the back, another in the belly, on the forehead. The priest called on God to help him as the Seven Deadly Sins danced around him, flying like tenacious wasps.

We are the happy vices,
We are the key to joy!

The censer continued to strike without ceasing. Father Nombrillet kept Floralie behind him, protecting her with his body, on which one could have stepped without his giving way. His strength came from Heaven. And his rage. He chastised in the name of a furious God.

Suddenly Anthyme recognized Floralie in her white gown. He pushed, shoved, threw people to the ground, tripped those who were in his way. He leaped into the cart to deliver Floralie from the dangerous madmen. Father Nombrillet saw him charge.

"The Devil has seven vices to serve him. If they aren't strong enough they call for the Devil himself," he explained.

And propelled by all the strength of his Catholic soul, the censer encountered the face of Anthyme.

"Vade retro Satanas," shouted the priest.

Roughly pushed by other demons summoned from Hell, the earth rose up like a wave, turned over and swallowed up, under terrestrial rubbish, all the living who had sinned. When he found the courage to open his eyes, Father Nombrillet understood that only the cart had been overturned by the too brutal exertion of the horses, who had given up under the whip of a maddened actor.

*   *   *

"Your village is so far," said Floralie.

"If you want to go back to your father's place it's that way," Anthyme indicated the direction, "but if you're coming with me, walk behind."

Father Nombrillet threw himself in front of them, his arms spread out, with the strength of someone who wants to prevent his brother from leaping over a precipice.

"No! God has set me in your path. You shall not pass! A man who meets God in his path should not pass without seeing him. I'll hear your confession because you are great sinners. If you do not purify your souls, they'll decompose like your bodies. Confess!"

Anthyme considered the threat of the censer.

"Save me, Father, but I have not sinned. You can believe me. I hardly smoke at all — only on Sunday afternoons and after supper. I never drink, but when I do I can tell you I don't get drunk very often. I get up early, I go to bed early, and I've never gone with a woman. Except today because it's my wedding day, and she's my wife. I'm poor like the good Lord wants French Canadians to be. I don't see how you can ask me for more than that."

"My son," shouted the priest, as angry as if he had been given a slap in the face, "be quiet! It's wrong to talk like that. Listen: you're a man and every man is a sinner."

"Fine," Anthyme conceded, "I accuse myself of being a man."

"Get on your knees; I'm going to forgive you."

Anthyme knelt, lowered his head and crossed his arms on his chest in the attitude of pious schoolboys. Father Nombrillet's hand, the same one that had torn open his face with a swing of the censer, was placed on his head. As he felt its gentle touch Anthyme realized that it was a protective hand, the hand of God.

"My son, you are forgiven. Get up now. God is within you."

Beneath Anthyme's feet the ground had become hard again because the earth likes the weight of an honest man.

"You, Blessed Virgin, follow me."

"She isn't the Blessed Virgin, she's my wife, Floralie."

"My son," interrupted Father Nombrillet, "the wife of a sinner is a sinner too. Come, so that I can forgive you. What thorn have you stuck in the head of Christ nailed to his cross?"

She objected. "I've never stuck a thorn in anybody's head."

"That's where you're wrong. The worst mistake is to be ignorant of your sins. Come."

Anthyme followed them.

"No, you stay there and pray that God won't send too many misfortunes onto this earth, where we all offend him so greatly."

Father Nombrillet had no lantern but because of the numerous fires crackling in the clearing the night had retreated a little, even if shadows were clouding the ground. Floralie walked behind the priest, who jumped up, stopped, murmured, stretched out his neck, looked for something and speeded up.

"Here, in the midst of so much sin, is the house of God."

Floralie saw, beneath the spruce, a little chapel made of squared-off tree-trunks. The bell-tower was lower than the surrounding trees and the roof was covered with branches. He pushed a silent door on its maple hinges.

"Come in."

The night, suddenly opaque, smelled of rotten earth and urine. There was so much night in the chapel that all the lanterns from the clearing would have been been drowned there. But Floralie could see very clearly the white face of Father Nombrillet. He slipped the bolt in the latch.

"My daughter, how many times have you sinned?"

Floralie reflected. She remembered the Italian.

The priest had come up to her. His breath smelled of potatoes.

"My daughter, is there no remorse squeezing your heart as if Satan's teeth were buried in it?"

She tried, with perfect goodwill, to feel the Devil's fangs in her heart.

"My daughter, if you feel no remorse, your heart is made of stone. Hearts of stone sink in Hell like stones in water."

" . . . "

"My daughter, all women are sinners."

She declared, "Yes, I have sinned."

Father Nombrillet leaped up. "You too!"

He unbuttoned the collar of his soutane, which was choking him.

"My daughter, let me suffer for your sin too. I share the agony of Christ in the Garden of Olives. Get on your knees."

He prayed. "My God, whose universe is fierce for the souls of your poor children. You put them in the world clothed in the white robes of the angels, but the world where you cast them is a stinking mudhole. My God, spare us, on the day of your most holy wrath."

Father Nombrillet gasped for breath.

"My God, your faithful servant is weary. You have given me my duty — to empty the sea of the sins that are inundating the earth — but just like Saint Augustine, you've only given me one bucket. I'm tired, Lord. Instead of continuing to empty the sea of sins, in your infinite mercy, which is even vaster than the sea of sins, instead of continuing to do the job you've demanded of me, I would like to let myself sink and drown like a sinner slowly drowning in his sin."

He tore off his soutane.

"But all you demons who cower like wolves, you won't get my soul, because God is with me!"

His ribcage was too narrow to contain his heart, swollen with a torrent of confused emotions.

"Pray, my daughter. The hour of God is at hand. Through my voice and my tongue he is asking you: is it with a man that you have sinned?"

Floralie had to accept the fact that the most precious joy that life had given her was wicked. Her soul could not drink deeply of it, on pain of death. On her knees before Father Nombrillet she was ready to regret every day of her life on which the thought of that joy had created some light.

"Yes," she confessed, "it was through a man that the Devil introduced me to joy."

"Ah! You too! And your soul?"

Father Nombrillet's voice was furious. When he knelt before her, so close to her, Floralie thought he was going to crush her in his arms as punishment for her sins.

"Man," roared the priest, "man corrupts everything he touches."

His hands seized Floralie's wrists, and his fingers were trembling.

"Did the man say, 'Take off your dress'?"

"Yes."

"And you took it off?"

"Yes."

"And God saw you in all the horror of your sin?"

The big lips of Father Nombrillet, like a frog, leaped, sputtering, onto Floralie's face.

"My daughter, admit your sin. You have allowed a man to put his hand here."

A feverish hand pressed Floralie's breast. She dared not push away the hand of God.

"Yes, he put his hand there."

"And you didn't push it away?"

"I didn't push it away."

"And it was good for you?"

Her numb lips could not articulate a single word.

Father Nombrillet panted and sweated. The night weighed on Floralie like a heavy, sweating man. Father Nombrillet trembled, his teeth chattering. A breath, almost a cry, surged from his mouth and resounded under the roof of the chapel. His head fell into Floralie's hair. After a long silence, during which he thought only of breathing, he said, "God and the Devil know that you are a great sinner. What penitence you will have to offer to God!"

And he put his shirt back on because he was afraid of catching cold.

*   *   *

An impatient bell rang several times. Slowly, in groups, the crowd headed towards the little chapel dedicated to the cult of the Holy Thorn. Soon they were pushing one another, none of them daring to hope they might have the privilege of entering the tiny chapel. They pushed with elbows and knees and shoved with their shoulders, lanterns colliding. The sick regained their strength for the combat that would bring them into the chapel, now all lit up, the shadows fleeing on the walls as the pilgrims insulted each other and prayed.

"Why don't they let us in in order of preference: first the dying, then the cripples, then the amputees, then the women and men and finally the children?"

"A sinner," retorted someone else, "has as much right to go in there as a sick person. A sinner is twice as important as a sick man."

"But there are sick people who are sinners too."

"They're entitled to go in before the others."

"I know a woman; she's dying, she's sick, she's a widow, she's paralysed, and apparently when she was young there wasn't a girl who knew how to sin like she did. I'd say she's the one that has the right to go in first."

"She's even got the right to sit in the Baby Jesus' cradle!"

"*I'd* say she's entitled to say Mass!"

"Shut up, you apostate; show some respect for holy things and pass the tobacco."

Soon it was impossible to get through the wall of backs. Inside, everyone was wedged into the hot, wet mud. They held their lanterns in their outstretched arms and a glaucous warmth spread through the crowd, where the noises from your neighbour's stomach seemed like your own and you could feel someone else's heart beat in your back. A single body in the chapel was sweating with a single fervour.

"My brothers, *adjuventutem totem nolem*: God is great, the Devil is powerful," cried Father Nombrillet above the mutterings of the crowd.

He had climbed onto a stump that served as a chair.

"Many of you have come here — God will bless you for it — and you know that the souls of the dead are even more numerous and that they are shoving each other too, trying to enter the kingdom of Heaven. But they must wait for the living, through their prayers and incessant mortifications, to force open the gates of Heaven where there reigns a God who is not generous but *just*. My brothers, you have come to observe the night of the Holy Thorn, that is to say the anniversary of the night nearly 2000 years ago — it was a spring night — when a naive, innocent, inoffensive little thorn was growing out of the ground and which, as it grew, became more and more wicked and only grew longer so that it would be sharp enough to sink into the head of Christ, our Saviour. It's a tradition for us to join together on this night of the Holy Thorn to remember that our lives are thorns buried in the head of God, because Christ is God, and to beseech him that, thanks to his forgiveness, Hell will not open beneath our feet like a trap-door in the floor to let you fall into the eternal fire. But nothing will protect you: you do not love God, my brothers, because you love women, alcohol which makes men like beasts, and perverted dances that bring the Devil among you. God wants you to love the spiritual and hate the material. Now, my brothers, you love too much what you can touch, what you can see, what you can taste. We might say that God created the soul while he left it to the Devil to create the body and the senses. I see you, I see the seal the demon's claw has inscribed on your foreheads. Throw yourselves on your knees and pray. The foot of God is upon your heads and only profound regret, confession and penitence will prevent his foot from pressing down and crushing you as in former times the Mother of God crushed the head of the serpent."

Father Nombrillet's sermon was interrupted by a cry. A fire had broken out among the pilgrims. Springing up from the earth, the fire took hold of clothes and held on. The pilgrims wept, pushed, shouted and hit one another. The fire tore off their clothes and scratched their faces. Impressed by Father Nombrillet's words a pious man had forgotten the lantern in his hand and it had fallen, spattering oil on a woman in front of him. Seized by the flames she had dropped her own lantern. They prayed and cursed and hit and trampled. They tore, but the human wall was impassable.

"God puts to the test those whom he has chosen," shouted Father Nombrillet.

The walls of the chapel opened and the flaming roof gave way and fell onto piles of blazing flesh.

Everywhere in the forest horses were running, trying to make the night extinguish the fire that was crackling in their frightened eyes.

When there was nothing left for its voracious jaws to graze on, the fire slept.

Then they began to look for the missing. The red ashes made a shroud that it was impossible to open, but the souls of the pilgrims who had died on this night of the Holy Thorn were ascending into Heaven. If the people's eyes had not been blinded by sin they would have seen them going towards the Eternal Father.

"The fire has sanctified them!"

"Father Nombrillet is the holiest of all."

Floralie, off to one side in the clearing, was crying. "I didn't confess all my sins to Father Nombrillet. I didn't have the strength. He'll be mad up in Heaven when he finds out I lied to him. His soul won't leave me in peace for a single night."

Pilgrims passing near her stopped to watch her cry.

"What's wrong, little girl?" asked an old man.

"I wish I'd been burned up like the others."

"Believe me, little one, it's better to be a flesh and blood girl than a saint of smoke and ashes. I'm old enough to know."

*   *   *

Anthyme had crossed the edge of the forest and he was dragging his heavy feet through a field. The clover was all wet from the night, which had barely ended.

"*Hostie!* I've seen Hell. It wasn't nice."

To forget what he had seen he recited bits of prayers, trying to think only of what he could see in front of his eyes: grass that was clean and neat as a woven blanket and trembling birch trees. But the fire he had seen coming out of the earth and the cries of the demons that had surged up with the fire would leave a horrible scar on his life. He would always remember this night, even when he had forgotten all the others.

His legs could carry him no further. He was too heavy a burden for himself. He stretched out in the clover.

His soul, he thought, left his body, buried itself in the ground, and having got a good grip went drifting up towards Heaven, spreading out in the sky like a beautiful tree. His soul had forgotten the fire of Hell and the memory, changed into leaves, murmured across the sky with a musical sound like water.

In the meadow, a woman's voice was calling, "Anthyme! Anthyme! My husband!"

He opened his eyes. Floralie was bending over him, but she seemed to be on a distant shore.

106

"Anthyme, your village is so far!"
He went back to sleep.

*   *   *

"Here they are!"
"I've found them!"
Cries of triumph made the delicate air of dawn burst out in the sky. The horse and carriage were cropping lightly the new grass.

Villagers, their shirts open and their hair dishevelled from the night's watch, their suits wrinkled, their clothes stained with beer, swooped down on Floralie and Anthyme. They were jubilant. They danced around the couple, swearing to show how happy they really were, to express the beauty of a man and woman entwined in the grass. They flung out obscene cries.

"We've been waiting for them while they were playing in the grass."

"If they spend all their nights counting the stars like that we can count on them, the race won't die out."

"They'll be the ones that wipe out the *maudits Anglais.*"

Laughter turned to hiccups. Floralie had heard everything but she had not yet opened her eyes.

"We spent the whole night waiting for them," a woman complained.

"In the name of God, do you think they were thinking about us? They only had thoughts for themselves!"

Awake, Anthyme smiled to see familiar faces around him, hairy, mussed up as though they had spent the night in the rain. They were holding their bellies, which hurt from so much laughing.

Anthyme and Floralie, sitting in the grass, looked at each other with the expression of people who haven't seen each other for a long time and are trying to bring past and present together in one face.

Revellers held their bottles over Floralie and Anthyme and spilled beer over their heads.

"Is it very far to your village now?" asked Floralie, on the verge of tears.

Hands seized them and lifted them into the carriage, the happy villagers getting in behind.

"Go on! Talk love talk to each other!"

Floralie spread her hand on her husband's arm.

"Anthyme?"

"Floralie?"

"I wonder if I was dreaming?"

"You should never dream."

THE AUTHOR

Roch Carrier was born in 1937 in a small village in the Appalachian Mountains. He studied in New Brunswick, Montreal and Paris. He now lives near Montreal with his wife and two daughters and teaches at the Université de Montréal.

A collection of short stories, *Contes pour mille oreilles*, and three novels have appeared in French. Two of these, *Floralie, Where Are You?* and *La Guerre, Yes Sir!* are available in English, translated by Sheila Fischman. His dramatic adaptation of *La Guerre, Yes Sir!* was performed in Montreal in the fall of 1970.